"A burglar," Daniel added, his voice still barely audible. "Someone who knew you wouldn't be in the house. He could have come in through the window and gone out through the back door."

Daniel was right. Why else would the back door be unlocked? Plus, she had put out word that she'd be in the barn tonight. She'd practically invited someone to break in.

Daniel went out of the office, back into the hall and headed for her bedroom. Her first thought was her jewelry box that would be sitting right on the dresser. She didn't have a lot, but there were several rings and a necklace that had once belonged to her mother and grandmother. That made Kara want to rush inside the room when Daniel opened the door.

But instead she froze in her tracks.

The lamp on the nightstand was on, the milky light practically spotlighting her bed. In the center of it was a woman with long brown hair. A stranger.

And her dead eyes stared up at the ceiling.

SAFEGUARDING THE SURROGATE

USA TODAY Bestselling Author

DELORES FOSSEN

Recycling programs for this product may not exist in your area.

ISBN-13: 978-1-335-55515-1

Safeguarding the Surrogate

This is a work of fiction. Names, characters, places and incidents are either the product of the author's imagination or are used fictitiously. Any resemblance to actual persons, living or dead, businesses, companies, events or locales is entirely coincidental.

This edition published by arrangement with Harlequin Books S.A.

For questions and comments about the quality of this book, please contact us at CustomerService@Harlequin.com.

Harlequin Enterprises ULC
22 Adelaide St. West, 40th Floor
Toronto, Ontario M5H 4E3, Canada
www.Harlequin.com

Printed in U.S.A.

Delores Fossen, a *USA TODAY* bestselling author, has written over one hundred novels, with millions of copies of her books in print worldwide. She's received a Booksellers' Best Award and an RT Reviewers' Choice Best Book Award. She was also a finalist for a prestigious RITA® Award. You can contact the author through her website at www.deloresfossen.com.

Books by Delores Fossen

Harlequin Intrigue

Mercy Ridge Lawmen

Her Child to Protect
Safeguarding the Surrogate

Longview Ridge Ranch

Safety Breach
A Threat to His Family
Settling an Old Score
His Brand of Justice

The Lawmen of McCall Canyon

Cowboy Above the Law
Finger on the Trigger
Lawman with a Cause
Under the Cowboy's Protection

HQN Books

Last Ride Texas

Spring at Saddle Run

Visit the Author Profile page at Harlequin.com.

CAST OF CHARACTERS

Deputy Daniel Logan—This Texas lawman is on the trail of a killer who's targeting former surrogates, including Kara Holland, the woman who carried his own child.

Kara Holland—She was the surrogate for Daniel and her dying sister, but now she finds herself in the crosshairs of a killer.

Sadie Logan—Daniel's eighteen-month-old daughter. She's too young to know she's in danger, but her father and Kara will do whatever it takes to keep her safe, even if they have to risk their own lives.

Eldon Stroud—Angry over losing his daughter. It's possible he's become so unstable that he's turned to killing.

Neal Rizzo—A local rancher with possible ties to a dangerous militia group. He could be using the murders to cover up his own criminal activity, or he could be the actual killer.

Sean Maynard—Kara's ex-boyfriend. He's not only bitter that Kara ended their relationship, he also despises Daniel. He might be after revenge.

Chapter One

Kara Holland stood in the darkness and waited for the killer.

With her heartbeat throbbing in her ears and her back pressed to the barn wall, she tried to listen for any sound to alert her that he was coming. Nothing. Not yet. But she'd done everything she could to lure him out and make him come after her.

And she was ready.

She had the Glock gripped in her hand, and thanks to the hours of firearms training, she knew how to use it. If that failed, if he somehow got the jump on her, she'd fall back on the hand-to-hand moves she'd also learned. Of course, those things didn't guarantee that she would stop him, but she had to try. She was tired of living with this smothering weight of fear.

Finally, she heard something. The sound of

a car engine. Then a door closing. He had finally come for her.

The next thing she heard were the footsteps, slow and cautious. They were coming straight toward her barn.

She'd purposely turned off all but the single light in the tack room, and Kara had left the door cracked just enough for a thin beam to pierce the darkness. She stayed in the shadows by a stack of hay bales, but when the killer came in the barn, she'd be able to see him.

Kara could certainly hear him.

Along with the footsteps, the hinges creaked on the barn door, and she pinpointed every bit of her focus while she lifted the Glock. And she took aim.

"Kara?" the man called out.

She groaned, mixing it with some muttered profanity, because she instantly recognized that voice. Not a killer. But Deputy Daniel Logan.

"What are you doing here?" she snapped once she could manage to speak.

"Checking on you," Daniel snapped right back.

When he stepped into that beam of light from the tack room, she had no trouble seeing the riled expression on his face. Or the rest of him for that matter. He was wearing his usual jeans and work shirt on his tall rangy body. His Mercy Ridge deputy's badge was clipped to his belt.

"I'm fine," Kara assured him. Of course, that wasn't true, and he could clearly see that. After all, she was waiting in her dark barn while holding a gun. "You can go."

"No, I won't." Daniel sounded "all cop" with that one-word response. And he didn't budge, either. In fact, he came closer, meeting her eye to eye.

"You shouldn't have come," Kara insisted.

"I wanted to have a look around and see for myself if the rumors were true. They are," he added in a snarl. "What the hell are you thinking?"

"You know what I'm thinking," she fired back.

That only caused him to release a long hard breath. No doubt one of frustration. Well, she was frustrated, too. And scared. Especially scared. Something that she'd hoped to end tonight.

"Two surrogates are dead," Kara reminded him. Not that a reminder was necessary. Daniel knew because she'd already told him. She'd taken the news articles to him right away when she had learned about the dead women. "Both used the Willingham Fertility Clinic in San Antonio."

Just as Kara had done. Again, no reminder was necessary for Daniel since the reason she had used the clinic and become a surrogate was to carry a baby for Daniel and his wife, Maryanne. Maryanne had also been Kara's sister.

As it always did, just remembering Maryanne made her feel as if someone had clamped a vise around her heart. It was almost certainly even worse for Daniel. It'd been nearly two years since Maryanne had lost her battle with breast cancer, but sometimes it felt as fresh as if it'd just happened.

When the grief came in these thick waves, Kara just reminded herself that she'd kept her promise to her sister. Kara had gone to the fertility clinic and used in vitro to get pregnant with Daniel and Maryanne's baby. The pregnancy and delivery had gone like clockwork, and Kara had given birth to a healthy baby girl, Sadie. But Maryanne had died four months before Sadie was born. Maryanne never got to hold the precious baby she'd so desperately wanted.

Now, the murders had happened. Murders

that added another layer of emotion to the grief. And that emotion was fear.

"First of all, there's no proof that the murders are connected to the Willingham Fertility Clinic," Daniel explained. He was definitely repeating himself since he'd tried to convince her of this before. "One of the women was likely killed by an abusive ex-boyfriend. The other is still listed as missing."

"There were signs of a struggle in the second woman's house," Kara quickly pointed out.

He nodded. "Even if she was attacked, that doesn't mean there's a link to the clinic." Daniel certainly sounded convinced of that, but…

"Yet you're here to check on me," she said. "You must think there's a credible threat or you wouldn't have come."

This time he scrubbed his hand over his face after he nodded again. "I'm a cop." He paused, his jaw muscles at war. "I'm your friend. And I'm worried about you. You said you thought someone was following you and watching you when you were shopping in San Antonio."

"Someone was." Kara was sure of that, but it hadn't been more than a gut feeling. "And I think someone got into my truck when I was there. The doors were unlocked, and I'm sure

I locked them. I could also tell someone had riffled through the glove compartment."

Daniel only sighed because they both knew that could have been a would-be thief. It wasn't that hard to break into a vehicle. "If you truly believe someone wants to kill you, then why the hell would you offer yourself up like this and try to draw him out?"

"Because I'm tired of being scared," she blurted out. Much to her disgust, her voice trembled. She hated that. "I've always been the strong one. No choice about that."

He nodded. "Because you had to take care of your sister after...well, after."

Daniel obviously hadn't wanted to blurt out what followed that "after," but he was talking about her parents being murdered. That'd happened when Kara had barely been eighteen, but she'd done a decent enough job raising Maryanne, who'd been three years younger. Heck, she had even continued to run the family ranch and had made it even more profitable than when her folks had been in charge.

The fear made her feel weak.

It made her feel like a coward.

"The second anniversary of Maryanne's death is coming up," Daniel said several moments later, "and I think it's just stirring up bad memories for you. It's certainly stirring up some for me," he added in a mumble.

Kara had no doubts about that. *None*. Daniel had loved her sister, and even though he hadn't approved of Maryanne opting for egg harvesting at a time when she should have been concentrating on her health and recovery, their marriage had held strong. Daniel had been as devastated by Maryanne's death as Kara had.

Daniel glanced around as if trying to figure out what to do, and his gaze came back to hers. "So, what was your plan? To let word get around that you'd be working in your barn, *alone*, for the next couple of nights. Then wait, hoping that a killer will come in here after you?"

Yes, that had been the plan, and Daniel had made it seem like a stupid one. It hadn't felt stupid, though, when she'd come up with it. However, it had felt desperate. Which it had been. This fear, and the threat, had to end.

"I've been having nightmares," she admitted. "Bad ones. And I couldn't get my mind off Brenda McGill and Marissa Rucker. Brenda's the surrogate who was found dead, and Marissa's the one who's missing."

Daniel made a sound to indicate that he understood that. "Then you started to dwell on the similarities between you and the women."

Again, the answer to that was yes, and there had indeed been similarities. Even Daniel couldn't deny that. Brenda and Marissa had both become surrogates to family members who'd had trouble carrying children. Both of them were brunettes—just like Kara. Both women had also lived in or near small towns. So did she. Kara lived on her horse ranch that was a good five miles from the town of Mercy Ridge where Daniel's own ranch was located.

"I know you don't believe this applies to my situation," she went on, "but there are fanatics out there. People who don't believe that surrogacy should be legal. The clinic admitted to me that they get threatening letters all the time. In one of them, the person said he was responsible for Brenda's death and that there'd be other murders."

None of that was an exaggeration, but as Kara heard her own words, she knew why Daniel was looking at her with what could only be sympathy in his otherwise cool gray eyes. Which, of course, only made her feel worse than she already did. Daniel shouldn't be here. His concern for her shouldn't have pulled him away from what he needed to be doing.

"You've obviously put in your usual shift at the sheriff's office, and you should be home with your daughter," Kara said. "How's Sadie?" she added, not only hoping to remind him that he should be on his way but also because she genuinely wanted to know.

The corner of his mouth lifted into a smile, but then he winced a little. "She repeated a bad word that she heard me say when I dropped my phone."

Sadie definitely was in the "little pitcher, big ears stage," and she was constantly babbling. She was also the spitting image of Daniel with her dark brown hair and smoky gray eyes. Just remembering the image of that precious little face caused Kara to relax some.

Daniel checked his watch. "Why don't you follow me home, and you can see Sadie for yourself? She should still be awake. And if you want, you can even stay the night in the guest room."

It was a nice offer, one that might not please Daniel's nanny, Noreen Ware, who was a stickler for keeping Sadie's routine. Still, Kara thought a glimpse of the baby might soothe the rest of her frayed nerves.

"Thank you," she muttered. "But just seeing Sadie should be enough. I won't stay long, and then I can come back here."

Daniel lifted an eyebrow. "Here as in the barn?"

"No. I'll stay in my house." With the doors locked and the security system armed. Kara tipped her head to the Glock she was holding by the side of her leg. "I'll put this in the house first."

Daniel walked out of the barn with her. "If you stay the night at my place, you could see Sadie in the morning and have breakfast with us."

He was obviously still concerned about her state of mind, and while spending time with Sadie and him was tempting, Kara pulled back a little. Something she always did when it came to Daniel. After all, he was an attractive man. Incredibly hot. Something she had been aware of since she'd been old enough to notice the opposite sex. But after Daniel had started dating Maryanne in high school, Kara had made sure to keep any tugs from the attraction in check. That was much harder to do when she was under the same roof with him.

"Thanks, but I'll just say good-night to Sadie and then come home," Kara answered, though she would still have to deal with the worry and fear that a killer had her in his sights. That's why she glanced around the backyard as they walked from the barn to her house.

Daniel looked around, too. The kind of glances a cop made. It eased some of the tightness in her chest to know that he hadn't outright dismissed her concerns, but there was still a good fifty feet between the house and the barn. That was plenty of space for a killer to come after her.

He made it up the back porch steps ahead of her, and when he reached for the doorknob, she realized he was going in with her. "You should lock your door," he commented when he opened it.

Kara froze. "I did." She took the keys from her jeans pocket to show him. "In fact, I've been making a point of locking up since I heard about the surrogates. I also use my security system when I'm sleeping." She hadn't turned it on, though, for her "stakeout" in the barn.

Daniel's forehead bunched up, but he certainly didn't freeze. He hooked his left arm around Kara, positioning her behind him, and in the same motion, he drew his gun. That sent her heartbeat into overdrive.

"You're sure you locked it?" he whispered.

"Positive."

He gave a quick nod. "Stay close and keep watch behind us."

That nearly robbed her of her breath, but Kara managed a nod, too. She was right behind Daniel when he stepped into her kitchen. As he'd done in the yard, his gaze fired all around, but he didn't go far. Only enough to get her inside, and then he eased the door shut behind them. That would prevent them from being ambushed. Well, hopefully it would.

But the killer could be anywhere in the house.

They waited there for what seemed to be an eternity, and Daniel lifted his head, obviously listening. Kara did the same, but the only thing she could hear was her too fast breaths. She tightened her grip on the Glock, hoping that would steady her suddenly raw nerves.

Her house was old and didn't have a modern open floorplan. That meant they couldn't see any of the other rooms from their position so that was probably why Daniel took several quiet steps to the side and peered into the kitchen.

"I don't see anyone," he whispered.

That didn't put her at ease because there were three bedrooms, a living and dining room, her office and two bathrooms. Plenty of places for someone to lie in wait for an attack.

Maybe the killer had gotten in and was now waiting to go after her. If so, he might not come out if he knew Daniel was there. Kara didn't want the guy to be able to stay in hiding. She wanted him out in the open so this showdown could take place. Then and only then would the danger finally be over.

Daniel motioned for her to follow him as he stepped into the kitchen. No one was there, and when she peered into the living room, she could see that the front door was shut, the chain lock still in place. Nothing in the room had been disturbed. It was just as she'd left it over an hour ago when she'd gone out to the barn. It was the same for the dining room when they went in there to look around.

Since the house only had one floor, Daniel headed to the hall next, and Kara was able to take in everything in a sweeping glance. All the bedroom doors and the one to her office and the hall bathroom were open. Just as they normally were. That meant Daniel and she would have to go into each room to make sure no one was there.

Daniel didn't waste any time doing just that. He went into the first guest room, his gaze shifting from one side of the room to the other. When they went inside, he checked the closet as Kara looked under the bed.

No one.

They repeated the process on the next bedroom and got the same results. However, the moment Daniel went through her office door, Kara knew something was wrong. The curtain was fluttering in the night breeze. And she soon saw why. The window was open.

Daniel didn't ask if she'd left it that way. Probably because like her, he saw the bits of glass on the floor. Someone had broken the window, slipped a hand through and unlocked it to get inside.

"Keep watch," Daniel reminded her, and he took out his phone to text for backup. Kara hadn't thought anything could rev up her heartbeat even more, but that did it.

While he waited for a response to his text, he glanced in every corner. The intruder wasn't here, and that left just one more place in the house. Her bedroom suite. Lots of places to hide in there, too.

His phone dinged, and Daniel checked the screen. "Barrett's on the way," Daniel told her in a whisper. "He'll be here in a few minutes."

Barrett was not only Daniel's brother, he was

also the town sheriff, and his ranch was only a couple of miles from Kara's place.

As she'd done in the other rooms, she looked around to see if anything was missing. And there was. Her laptop was gone, and the bottom drawer of her desk was open. The small metal box she kept there was also open, and the money that would have normally been inside was missing.

"A burglar," Daniel added, his voice still barely audible. "Someone who knew you wouldn't be in the house. He could have come in through the window and gone out through the back door."

Daniel was right. Why else would the back door be unlocked? Plus, she had put out word that she'd be in the barn tonight. And that made Kara want to kick herself. She'd practically invited someone to break in.

With Kara right behind him, Daniel went out of the office, back into the hall and headed for her bedroom. Her first thought was her jewelry box that would be sitting right on the dresser. She didn't have a lot, but there were several rings and a necklace that had once belonged to her mother and grandmother. That made Kara want to rush inside the room when Daniel walked through the door.

But instead she froze in her tracks.

The lamp on the nightstand was on, the milky light practically spotlighting her bed. In the center of it was a woman with long brown hair. A stranger.

And her dead eyes stared up at the ceiling.

Chapter Two

Daniel felt the quick punch of shock and dread before his instincts kicked in, and he pushed Kara behind him. He definitely didn't want her touching the body and contaminating the scene, but there was a bigger concern here.

The killer could still be in the room.

No way could he leave Kara alone, so he nudged her with his elbow and tipped his head to the closet and adjoining bathroom to let her know he had to check them out. She gave a shaky nod, and she started walking when he did, but she didn't take her eyes off the dead woman.

Kara was as tough as nails. He knew that. And she'd even been with Maryanne when she drew her last breath. They both were. But murder was different, and even though Daniel hadn't had a chance to examine the body, he figured this was a homicide.

Moving as fast as he could, he went to the closet. No one was lurking in there. Next up was the bathroom, and he held his breath until he threw back the shower curtain. No killer there, either. In fact, the only signs of one were the office and the bedroom.

"Do you know the dead woman?" Daniel asked Kara once he had her back in the bedroom.

Kara shook her head, and the breath she dragged in was shaky, long and hard. He wasn't sure if it was a good thing or not that this was a stranger. If it was someone she knew, it might make it easier to figure out how she'd gotten here and why she'd died. But he knew from personal experience that it could crush you to lose someone you knew.

Maryanne's death had certainly crushed him.

"Why is…*was* she here?" Kara asked. Her voice was ragged and with hardly any sound. Because her arm was right against his, Daniel could feel her muscles trembling.

Daniel wanted to get started on answering that *why* question so he motioned for Kara to stay put, and he went closer to the bed. He didn't recognize the woman, either, but he made a mental description of her. Brown hair, brown eyes, slim build, midtwenties. She was wearing a yellow dress. And jewelry. Gold earrings, a heart necklace and three rings. Apparently, the person who'd put her here hadn't seen fit to rob her.

There were bruises on her wrists and what appeared to be a puncture mark on her right forearm. Maybe from a syringe. If so, it was fresh, and it could mean she'd been drugged.

When Daniel moved to the other side of the bed, he saw something lying next to her. It was a Texas driver's license, and without touching it, he leaned in to see the name on it.

"Mandy Vera," he relayed to Kara. "According to her address, she's from San Antonio."

Kara repeated the name several times, but then she shook her head. "It's not familiar. How did she get here?"

Daniel wasn't sure, but judging from those bruises, she hadn't come willingly. However, before he could consider more than that, he heard a vehicle pull up in front of the house. Seconds later, there was a knock at the door.

"It's me," Barrett called out.

Good. Because Daniel not only needed backup, he also wanted his brother to take charge of the crime scene so that he could get Kara out of there. After all, the killer could still be hanging around. And that made Daniel want to curse. Kara had tried to make herself bait, and it could have worked. She could have been the one to end up dead in that bed.

With Kara still close to him, Daniel went to the door and opened it. He didn't offer any explanation to Barrett. Daniel just motioned for him to follow them back to the bedroom. With a puzzled look on his face, Barrett stepped in. Then he froze for a second before he went to the body.

"What the hell happened?" Barrett demanded.

"Not sure. Kara and I came in from the barn and found her like this. The window's broken in Kara's office so that appears to be the point of entry. It's just up the hall, and there are some items missing."

Daniel immediately saw the questions in his brother's eyes. Eyes that were a genetic copy of his own.

"You didn't see who did this?" Barrett asked, aiming that question at Kara.

She shook her head, pushing the wisps of her dark brown hair from her face. "No. I was in the barn when Daniel got here."

"She was trying to draw out the killer," Daniel supplied.

No need for him to add more to that because Daniel and Barrett had already discussed Kara's obsession with a possible surrogate killer. And here he hadn't even believed there was a killer.

Well, he sure as heck believed it now.

Of course, he had to stay objective and look into the possibility that this wasn't connected to anything to do with surrogacies. If it wasn't, then it would give them another puzzle as to why this had happened. But one thing was for certain, it was connected to Kara. Someone had gone to a lot of trouble to stage a crime scene like this. There had to be a reason for that, and Daniel would make it his priority to figure that out.

Along with keeping Kara safe.

"So, if the killer came through the office window, how'd he get her in here in the bedroom?" Barrett muttered. "He must have broken in and unlocked the back door to bring in the body."

"I only heard Daniel's truck when he drove up," Kara said. "And yours. I didn't hear another vehicle."

"How long were you in the barn?" Daniel asked her.

She had clamped her teeth over her bottom lip and had to release it before she spoke. "Over an hour."

Plenty of time for someone to do this. "The killer could have parked on a nearby ranch trail, walked to the house with the woman, broken in and then murdered her."

Barrett nodded. "If so, there could be footprints or tracks. I'll get a CSI team and the medical examiner out here right away."

Daniel took out his phone as well, and he checked the time. The Willingham Fertility Clinic was already closed for the night so he called his contact Loretta Eaton, the office manager. He wasn't sure how much info Loretta could give him without a search warrant, but this was a start.

"Mandy Vera," Daniel said to Loretta after he identified himself. "I'm pretty sure she was just murdered, and her body was left here in Mercy Ridge." Though he'd have to verify that her driver's license wasn't a fake. "I need to know if she had any connection whatsoever to Willingham."

Loretta's sharp sound of shock made Daniel wish he'd sugarcoated that just a little. Of course, it was impossible to sugarcoat murder.

"Her name doesn't ring any bells. I'm home

right now and don't have access to the files," she said, "but I'll go into the clinic and check."

"Thanks. Text me as soon as you know one way or another."

"I will. Uh, how was this woman killed?" Loretta asked.

Daniel had no intention of giving her any other details. Not until he figured out who was responsible for this. Probably not Loretta, though. The woman was in her midsixties and petite. Still, she might say something to the wrong person.

"I can't get into that right now," Daniel answered. "But it'd help a lot if you check those records for that name."

Loretta repeated her assurance that she would, and Daniel ended the call. Barrett, too, had finished his call and was studying the body.

"The ME will have to confirm it, but it looks like strangulation," Barrett said. "There doesn't appear to be any blood or tissue under her nails."

Daniel had noticed that as well, and that likely meant Mandy hadn't struggled while she was being strangled. Maybe because she'd been too drugged to do anything to stop the attack. Or maybe her killer had worn gloves and long sleeves. But Daniel figured if the woman had been conscious, she would have definitely fought back, and the covers on the bed didn't appear to have been disturbed.

"There are marks on her forearm," Daniel explained. "It could have been the way the killer got the drugs into her."

Barrett made a sound of agreement, and when he kept his attention on Kara, it caused Daniel to look back at her. There wasn't much more color in her face than there was the dead woman's, and the pupils of her dark brown eyes were too large. She looked as if she might be in shock. No surprise there. However, it was a reminder that she shouldn't be here.

"I can't have you pack anything to take with you," Daniel told her. "Everything in the house has to be treated as a crime scene."

He followed her gaze as it drifted over his shoulder to the framed photo of Sadie and him that she had on her dresser. Daniel knew that she loved Sadie, but there were plenty of photos of just his little girl and even some with Kara and Sadie. He wasn't sure why her choice of pictures unsettled him, but what was more unsettling was the look in her eyes when their gazes met. She quickly turned from him, as if she hadn't wanted to give away what she was thinking.

Or feeling.

Hell. He wasn't stupid, and he'd felt that tug inside him sometimes when he looked at Kara. A tug he hadn't wanted, but it was just a basic primal urge. After all, she was an attractive woman. However, Daniel hadn't wanted her to feel that same attraction for him.

"You okay?" Barrett asked, and that's when Daniel realized his brother was volleying glances at Kara and him.

"Fine," they answered in unison. Which, of course, only made them sound guilty of something.

"Fine," Daniel repeated, changing his tone so that he sounded like a cop. Thankfully, he didn't have to add more because he heard a familiar voice at the front door.

"It's me," someone called out. Leo, his kid brother and fellow deputy.

"We're back here," Barrett told him.

Several seconds later, Leo appeared in the doorway, and as Daniel and Barrett had done, his gaze swept around the room. Blowing out a slow breath, he put his hands on his hips. "Damn," he grumbled.

That about summed up how Daniel was feeling, but his brother's arrival was good news. Now, he wouldn't have to wait around to get Kara out of there.

"I'm taking Kara to my house," Daniel explained. That would accomplish a couple of things. She wouldn't have to keep staring at the body, and he could check on Sadie. He had a good security system, but he'd feel better once he was sure the nanny and his daughter were okay.

Barrett nodded. "Walk with them to Daniel's truck," he added to Leo.

Kara made a soft groan, one that had come from deep within her chest. No way had she forgotten that a killer had been here, but maybe it had just occurred to her that he could still be lurking around.

She didn't resist when Daniel took hold of her arm to guide her out of the room, but she did look back at the dead woman. "We have to find out who did this. We have to stop him."

The *we* concerned Daniel a lot, and it caused Leo to give him a raised questioning eyebrow. No way did Daniel want Kara involved in this investigation. But she already was. The trick would be to keep her safe and not allow her to set herself up as bait again.

"You're taking her to your place?" Leo asked when they reached the front door.

Daniel nodded, but he felt the split second of hesitation in Kara. He didn't want to read too much into it. After all, before they'd found the body, he'd already talked her into going to his house to say good-night to Sadie. But this would be more than just her popping in. It was going to take a day or two for the CSI team to process the scene. Only then would Kara be free to return.

The question was—would she want to go back? Would she ever be able to walk into her bedroom and not see the woman's dead body? If the answers to those questions were no, then she might be at his place longer than either of them wanted.

When they went out the door and onto the porch, Daniel immediately looked around for any signs of the killer. Nothing. There were no trampled down plants or grass. Leo was doing the same thing, and he used the flashlight function on his phone to examine the gravel and dirt driveway in front of the house where Barrett, Daniel and he were all parked.

Still nothing.

Of course, he could have screwed up any prints when he'd driven in. It hadn't been on

Daniel's radar that a killer could have just been there. Just the opposite. He'd come to tell Kara that there was no reason for her to lure out a killer who didn't exist. Now he knew differently and wondered how soon it would be before Kara said *I told you so.*

Or blamed him for this.

If he'd just listened to her, there might not be a dead woman lying on her bed. He might have been staking out her place and could have caught the guy red-handed.

"I'll have to come back in the morning to check on the horses," Kara muttered as Daniel helped her into his truck.

Her comment actually made him feel better because it meant the shock was wearing off. "I'll have one of my ranch hands do it."

Daniel had four who worked for him, managing the herds of Angus cattle that he raised, and he'd send one of them here to her place. No way did he want Kara out in the open like that until they had some answers. He was pretty sure those answers would confirm something he already felt in his gut.

That Kara was in danger.

With that unsettling thought going through his head, Daniel started his truck as Leo headed back to the house. Daniel would have driven away had his phone not buzzed with a call. When he saw the name on the screen, he knew he had to take the call right away.

"It's Loretta Eaton from the fertility clinic," he relayed to Kara, and he hit the answer button while he continued to keep watch around them.

"Oh, God," Loretta immediately said. And Daniel felt that same avalanche of dread that he heard in the woman's voice. "It's true, Deputy Logan. God, it's true. Mandy Vera was one of our surrogates."

Chapter Three

Kara didn't have to hear what Loretta had said to Daniel. She could tell from his softly muttered profanity and the grim look on his face that what the woman from the fertility clinic had told him wasn't good news.

"Thanks for letting me now. I can't talk right now. I'll call you tomorrow," Daniel told Loretta, and he ended the call.

"Mandy was a surrogate," Kara stated.

Daniel hesitated for several moments before he nodded, and he fired off a text. "I'm letting Barrett know. He'll want someone from SAPD to go out to Mandy's place and have a look around."

Yes, and maybe they would find something, especially if that's where the killer had gotten his hands on the woman. But if that's where it'd happened, then why hadn't he just murdered her there?

The answer to that settled like ice in her bones.

"This is personal," Kara managed to say. "He set all of this up to taunt me."

Daniel didn't deny it. Couldn't. Because he knew as well as she did that there was no other logical reason for why Mandy had been brought here and posed liked that in Kara's bed. It had all been set up to shock and terrify her. And it had worked. The fear slid through her, breath to bone.

But so did the anger.

Kara had felt plenty of anger when she'd set her plan of bait into motion. She hadn't wanted to feel helpless, and she'd gone into that barn, waiting for the worst to happen. However, the anger she'd felt then was a drop in the bucket compared to what she felt now. The monster who'd murdered Brenda and now Mandy wasn't going to get away with this.

"I didn't hear anything about the killer posing Brenda's body or moving it to a location away from the place she was killed," Kara said as Daniel drove away from her house. "You read the police reports. Was there any mention of that?"

Even in the dim light from the dashboard panel, she could see the rock-hard set of his jaw muscles. He was still glancing around, no doubt looking for the person who'd murdered Mandy. "None." This time when he cursed, it wasn't muttered. "I didn't believe you. I didn't believe there was a killer."

She heard the guilt in his voice and knew this was something that would eat away at him. But Kara had no intention of holding his feet to the fire on this.

"You had to look at this as a cop," she reminded him. Like Daniel, she also continued to keep watch, but there were lots of woods on the rural roads between their two ranches. "Besides, there wasn't a lot of evidence to convince you that someone was targeting surrogates."

"You knew there was a killer," he snapped.

It wasn't much consolation for her to know that she'd been right all along about her being in the crosshairs of a killer. "Because I sensed someone following me. Because I was paranoid," she added in frustration. "I've been paranoid for the past thirteen years."

He didn't have to ask what had happened thirteen years ago to make her that way. Daniel knew. That's when her parents had been murdered. But not just murdered. A ranch hand her father had fired, Lamar Darnell, had stalked her parents and taunted them with threats for weeks. Before the cops could find Lamar and arrest him, he'd shot and murdered her mom and dad and then turned the gun on himself.

There was that old saying that what didn't kill you made you stronger. Well, their deaths hadn't killed her, but Kara had known she wouldn't go through something like that again without a fight. For all the good it'd done.

A woman was still dead.

"I should have handled this a different way," Kara whispered, talking to herself. "I should have tried to find out the names of the surrogates so I could contact them and warn them. I should have looked harder to find some kind of evidence to give the San Antonio cops a push to get involved."

Daniel groaned, and he shook his head. "If you need to blame someone, blame me. I didn't listen, but I'm listening now. Whoever's doing this might have a beef against the fertility clinic. Maybe against the idea of surrogacy itself. Either way, I want access to the files. I want to read some of that letter they got from the guy claiming to have killed Brenda."

Kara wanted that, as well. In fact, she'd asked for permission to read that letter and any others of a threatening nature, but her request had been denied. Maybe Daniel could use his badge to get to them, and that in turn could lead them to suspects.

Maybe an insane one.

"Mandy was a brunette, too," Kara murmured, and just that little detail caused her stomach to twist into knots. "Just like Brenda and Marissa. Just like me."

"Yes," Daniel said, and he paused for several moments. "Often a killer like this will stick to the same type of victim and the same method of murder."

Kara thought about that. Brenda had been beaten to death, and from the looks of it, Mandy had been strangled. They still didn't know what had happened to the missing woman, Marissa, but Kara had the sickening feeling that they'd find her dead, too. And everything was pointing to their being surrogates at the same clinic as the reason for their deaths.

"You think there's more than one killer?" she asked, trying to focus on the investigation rather than the images of the dead woman.

Daniel lifted his shoulder. "It's too early to say. Maybe. Or maybe he just got carried away with Brenda. He could have beaten her because she fought back."

True, and that didn't ease the stomach knots

any. It only proved to her that whoever was doing this would use any means to reach his goal.

And his goal was to kill.

"All the surrogates who used that clinic will need to be contacted," Kara said. "They should know there's a possible threat."

He made a sound of agreement. "It's tricky when getting access to medical records, but maybe the press can help with that. When the news media picks up on the two murders, possibly three, and all were former patients at Willingham, then—"

When he didn't finish that, Kara turned to him and saw that he was looking in the rear-view mirror. At first, she didn't see anything other than the darkness, but then she spotted the vehicle.

A black truck with the headlights off.

"It just pulled out from a side road," Daniel said.

Kara's heart immediately jumped to her throat. There were other ranches and houses out here, and while there wasn't a lot of traffic, there was still some. Still, everything inside her went on alert because this could be the killer, especially considering the driver wasn't using the headlights.

Without looking at her, Daniel passed his

phone to her. "Text Barrett and let him know that we're being followed."

Kara tamped down her nerves and did as Daniel asked. She also kept her attention nailed to the side mirror so she could see the truck. The driver still had the headlights off, and they stayed that way even after Daniel flashed his own lights. Even though the truck was behind him, he'd be able to see the lights go on and off.

Despite the fact that Kara had been expecting a reply from Barrett, the dinging sound from Daniel's phone nearly had her shifting her gun to take aim. "Barrett's on the way," she relayed to him.

Kara did a quick estimate and figured Daniel's brother could be there in five minutes or so. Then, maybe they could stop the truck and figure out what was going on. It could turn out to be nothing. Or this could be a huge break. One that would lead them to catching a killer.

"I don't want to go to my place just yet," Daniel muttered.

"I agree." Kara couldn't say that fast enough. If this was a killer, no way did she want him going to Daniel's doorstep. Sadie was in the house, and if there was trouble, she could be hurt.

That reminder gave Kara a new surge of

anger that steadied her hands and her mind. She'd already lost too many people she loved, and she would do whatever she needed to do to stop it from happening again.

"He lowered his window," Daniel said, his voice hard and tight. He drew his weapon while he continued to drive. "Get down on the seat."

Kara wanted to argue with him, to remind him that she could help him keep watch. But this wasn't the time to distract Daniel with what would no doubt be a disagreement. The cop in him wouldn't want her to take any unnecessary risks—even if he was taking one just by staying behind the wheel.

The reality of that risk hit her hard when she saw the hand snaking out from the open window of the truck. Oh, mercy. The driver had a gun.

And he aimed it right at them.

She slid lower into the seat but not so low that she wouldn't be able to provide backup. And she did that just as the bullet slammed into Daniel's truck. The sound she heard was of metal ripping into metal. Not once but three times. That sent her heart pounding and her grip tightening on her Glock.

"Hold on," Daniel ground out, and he hit the accelerator.

This wasn't exactly a good road for speeding. There were a lot of curves, even a bridge, and it would be so easy for them to crash. Still, they needed to get out of range of those bullets.

"Text Barrett again," Daniel told her. "Tell him we're under fire."

Before Kara could do that, the sound of another shot blasted through the air. This one didn't hit Daniel's truck, but the shooter immediately sent another shot their way. Then another. Worse, the guy was managing to keep up with them. Both trucks were flying down the country road.

She sent the text, knowing that at the speed they were going, it would take Barrett even longer to reach them. However, he could likely manage to get them some backup that could arrive faster since they were headed in the direction of Mercy Ridge.

Daniel sped past the turn that would have taken them to his ranch, and then he cursed. Kara risked sitting farther up in the seat so she could look in the side mirror again. What she saw sent her heart to her knees. The shooter had slowed down and taken that turn.

He was heading to Daniel's ranch.

Daniel slammed on the brakes, the tires squealing against the asphalt, and he turned his truck around. Not easily and not fast. It was hard to do a U-turn on such a narrow road, and the maneuver ate up precious seconds, but Daniel finally got them turned around.

"Call Noreen," Daniel snapped, but Kara was already doing that.

With the lead the driver of the truck had on them, he would make it to the ranch before they did. Kara tried not to let that terrify her. Terror wouldn't help right now. She just needed to let the nanny know what was going on so she could do whatever possible to keep a killer from getting into the house.

Thankfully, Noreen answered on the first ring, and Kara didn't even bother easing into this. "There's trouble. A gunman is on the way to the ranch," Kara blurted out.

"Kara?" Noreen said. "Why are you calling? What's going on?"

"I don't have time to explain everything. He'll be there within minutes so you need to make sure all the windows and doors are locked. Turn on the security system if it's not already on and then take Sadie into one of the bathrooms. Do it now," Kara snapped when Noreen didn't respond.

"I'm checking the doors." Noreen finally said. "God, what's happening?"

"We're not sure, but this gunman could try to break in. Are the doors and windows locked?"

"Oh, God," Noreen repeated. "We keep the windows locked, and the doors are, too." Kara heard some soft clicks. "And I've just set the security system."

"Stay on the line and get Sadie to the bathroom," Kara instructed.

Daniel muttered something, maybe a prayer, and he continued to speed through the night toward the ranch. She could hear their gusting breaths, but that was the only sound.

Until the next shot.

It seemed to come out of the blue, and it blasted through the window right next to her head. The safety glass tumbled down onto her, and Kara didn't even have time to bring up her gun before the gunman fired another bullet. Then another.

"Get down," Daniel yelled.

She did but not before she saw the black truck. Not on the road ahead of them. The driver had pulled off onto a trail, the front of the truck facing them.

With a hail of bullets coming directly at

them, Daniel's truck lurched to the right, and that's when Kara knew their situation had gone from bad to worse. Because the gunman had managed to shoot out at least one of the tires.

Fighting with the steering wheel, Daniel kept going, and the bullets kept coming. The shooter's truck did, too. From the glimpse that Kara got in the side mirror, the driver had bolted out behind them again. And that meant they were now headed for Daniel's ranch.

"Do you have Sadie in the bathroom?" Kara asked Noreen.

"Yes." Noreen's voice sounded even shakier than it had before.

Kara could also hear Sadie fussing, and that was like a fisted hand on her heart. Sadie could be afraid. She was too young to understand what was going on, but the little girl had no doubt picked up on her nanny's fear.

The shots started again, and Daniel's truck did another lurch. Mercy, the gunman was trying to stop them, and if he succeeded, they'd be sitting ducks. He could continue to fire until he killed them both.

"I'm not going closer to the house," Daniel snarled.

Unlike Noreen, there was no fear in his voice. Just some raw anger. Something Kara totally understood. She wanted to make this gunman pay hard for what he was doing.

"Text Barrett again and give him our location," Daniel added, and he finally brought his truck to a stop.

Kara knew that it was necessary for Barrett to know where they were so that there wouldn't be the possibility of being wounded by friendly fire, but she wanted to help Daniel with this showdown. Still, she sent off the text, tossed the phone onto the glass-strewn seat and levered herself up so that she could return fire. Beside her, Daniel did the same.

There was another sound. Not gunfire this time. But rather the gunman throwing his truck into Reverse. He flew backward, whipping the truck onto a trail so that he could turn around.

Daniel bolted out from cover, taking aim, and he fired two rounds into the cab of the truck. However, it was already too late.

The killer was speeding away.

Chapter Four

While Daniel waited for an update from Barrett, he paced across his living room and watched Kara. He had to hand it to her—she was looking a lot steadier than she must be feeling.

And she was doing that for Sadie's sake.

Kara was pulling off the steady facade, too, because Sadie showed no signs that anything was wrong while Kara read her a story. They were snuggled up on the sofa with Sadie in her lap. Of course, Sadie was only eighteen months old and thankfully too young to realize something bad had happened.

The calm veneer wouldn't last for Kara, though. Daniel was certain of that because he figured it wouldn't last for him, either. Right now, he had plenty to do, what with trying to find out what the hell had happened with that attack, but once Sadie was in bed and Kara and he started talking about it, the emotions would be right there at the surface.

The fear, too.

After all, their attacker was still at large, which meant he could return for another round. Since the shooter was also likely the same person who'd murdered Mandy, it wouldn't be a friendly encounter.

Sadie clapped when Kara finished the book and gave Kara a kiss on the cheek. That was Noreen's cue to get Sadie moving. The nanny was also keeping up appearances, trying not to let it show that she was worried, but Daniel would have to talk to her soon, too, and try to reassure her that he'd do whatever it took to keep them all safe.

"Remember, you get to sleep in the bathtub," Daniel told Sadie.

That caused his daughter to grin. She believed this was some kind of an adventure. Like indoor camping with the bedding that he'd put in the tub for her. However, it was much more than an adventure. It was for her own safety. If a gunman fired shots, Sadie would be safer in the tub than in her crib. Daniel would add a level to that safety by sleeping on the bathroom floor next to her.

As usual, Sadie doled out good-night kisses

and hugs first to Kara and then to Daniel. He let the hug linger a couple of moments. Just having his baby with him settled him down a little. However, it also reminded him of how high the stakes were right now. His little girl could be in danger, and he needed to find out why because the why often led to the who.

"What kind of updates have you been getting?" Kara asked the moment Sadie and Noreen were out of earshot.

Obviously, Kara had noticed that during the time she'd been reading to Sadie, he'd been getting texts. Some had been from Barrett, others from Leo, but neither of them had good news.

"There's still no sign of the killer," he said, giving her the worst of it first. Until they found him, they couldn't make an arrest, and the threat would continue.

Kara nodded, and she stayed quiet a moment, no doubt trying to come to terms with that. "Anything on Mandy?"

"Some, most of it is still preliminary, though. Cause of death is likely strangulation. San Antonio PD is going through her place now, and they've told us there are signs of a struggle."

Another nod from Kara, followed by some deep breaths. She was trying to steady herself.

Good. Because even though she had a darn good reason to fall apart right now, Daniel was hoping she wouldn't. He needed both of them to hold things together so they could figure out the safe thing to do about Sadie. About Kara, too, since she was almost certainly the killer's target.

But why hadn't the guy just killed her tonight?

Kara had put out the word that she'd be in the barn, and he could have gone in there after her. It could be this was some kind of cat-and-mouse game, or maybe the killer was a coward. It was one thing to take and drug an unarmed woman like Mandy, but he must have known that Kara would be armed and ready for him.

"The crime scene unit is out at your house," he went on after glancing through his texts. "They've found two sets of footprints outside your office window. There are some drag marks, too. So maybe the guy had drugged Mandy before he got there, revived her enough so she could walk at least part of the way and then gave her a second dose of the drug once he got her inside."

Of course, the killer could have incapacitated the woman other ways, smothering or a blow to the head, but it didn't really matter.

He'd gotten Mandy into Kara's house, murdered her and staged the body. Maybe as a threat to Kara to tell her to back off her investigation into the missing and dead surrogates, maybe just to torment her.

The tormenting was definitely working.

She shook her head. "I didn't hear anything to let me know someone was in my house."

At the moment, he considered that a good thing. "If you had, you might have gone inside to check things out and been killed."

Daniel hoped that was a warning she'd take to heart. He didn't want Kara setting up any more traps for this snake. She certainly didn't jump to defend what she'd done. Nope. Her emotions went in the other direction. Her eyes filled with tears.

"Oh, God. Daniel, I'm so sorry."

Hell. He'd hoped she would be able to keep the aftermath of all of this at bay. Apparently not. Those tears didn't spill down her cheeks, but she was blinking hard to keep them from falling.

Daniel figured this was a mistake the size of Texas, but he went to her and pulled her into his arms. Kara practically sagged against him, her head landing on his shoulder. He didn't want to notice how well she fit. Didn't want to notice her scent that he immediately took in. Or the soft breathy sigh she made.

But he noticed.

Having her this close was a reminder that she was an attractive woman. And that he was a man. Something he'd been noticing more and more whenever he was around Kara.

It'd been nearly two years since he'd lost his wife. Since Kara had lost her sister. It was only natural for Kara and him to tap into the grief they shared for the loved one they'd lost. Grief that could still slice to the bone.

Added to that, there was Sadie. Kara had carried his little girl for nine months, and Sadie and she had DNA in common. These were all the things that Daniel had gone over and over. All the reasons he kept giving himself for why he felt this connection with Kara. At the moment, though, those were not the reasons his body was having this reaction to her.

A bad reaction.

He felt the stir of familiar heat and knew if he let it continue that it would put a serious dent in his resolve to keep his hands off his late wife's sister. Sexual heat could do that. It could make excuses and blur lines that shouldn't be blurred.

And that's why Daniel stepped back from her.

He'd hoped that Kara was so caught up in her near meltdown that she wouldn't notice how fast he'd moved away from her. But she did notice. Her eyes came to his, their gazes connecting, and he saw something he wished weren't there.

The same blasted heat that he was battling. Kara was battling it as well, and in that long look they gave each other, many things passed between them. Things best left unsaid, and that's why Daniel decided to do something to put an end to this nonverbal conversation.

He went into the adjacent kitchen to get himself a bottle of water. What he really wanted was a beer or a shot of something stronger, but until the killer was caught, he was essentially on the job. Plus, he didn't want anything, including this lust for Kara, to cloud his head and therefore his judgment.

"How secure are the grounds around your ranch?" Kara asked, joining him in the kitchen.

She didn't look at him. A smart decision. That meant she'd learned her lesson about making long eye contact with him. Added to that, it was a good question. Too bad his answer was going to suck. He considered softening it some, but that could end up being dangerous. He didn't want Kara to have a false sense of safety that could end up getting her killed.

"I have four hundred acres," he reminded her. "Along with barns and other outbuildings. There are at least a half-dozen old trails that thread through the area. And in the middle of all that sits this house."

She nodded, drew in another of those unsteady breaths. "I've brought danger to your house, to your daughter."

"Wrong. The killer did that by going after us tonight." He paused, added the rest that she needed to hear. "I could have been the target."

Now it was surprise that flashed through her eyes. "You?"

"Me," he verified, and he tapped his badge to let her know that he was referring to his being a cop. "I've arrested people who might want to get back at me."

In fact, just a couple of months ago he'd had a tense run-in with a nearby rancher, Neal Rizzo, who'd threatened him. Mandy's murder pointed to the other surrogates and the fertility clinic, but Daniel had to look at this from all angles. And one big angle was that Mandy's killer hadn't launched another attack until after Kara and he had left for his ranch. It would have been easier for the killer just to go after her when she was alone. But he hadn't. So, maybe Kara and he were both targets.

"I'm going through all my old cases," he went on. He'd have a chat with Rizzo, too. "We'll take as many precautions as we can."

They'd already done that by closing all the curtains and blinds, locking all the doors and arming the security system. He also had several full-time ranch hands and another part-time one who could help keep an eye on the house and grounds. But even all of that might not be enough.

"There are just too many places for someone to lie in wait," Daniel continued a moment later. "Or someone could climb up one of the trees and take shots at the house. That's why Noreen will be sleeping in her bathroom tonight, and you'll be staying in the guest bathtub. It won't be especially comfortable, but it'll add another safety layer."

Kara didn't give him even an argumentative glance about that. "You'll take precautions, too?"

He nodded. "No pj's for me tonight." Though he was more of a "boxers and tee" kind of guy, and in his earlier days, commando. "I'll be wearing Kevlar." And he'd be armed to the hilt. He didn't like carrying a gun with Sadie around, but he couldn't risk having to run for his weapon if the worst happened. "Keep your Glock with you."

She nodded as if that were exactly what she'd expected him to say, but Daniel could still see the tension, and the fear, this had caused her. Tension and fear, though, were better than not being prepared if this killer came after them again.

"Because it's already getting late, we need to stay here for the night," Daniel went on, "but tomorrow, I'll find someplace safer." He'd been mulling that over, while no place was a 100 percent safe, he had an idea. "I'm considering moving the four of us to the Serenity Inn in town."

The inn was on Main Street, only two buildings away from the sheriff's office. Along with having a security system and motion-activated exterior lights, the open yard would make it harder for a gunman to sneak onto the grounds.

Harder but not impossible.

"I'm sure I can talk Ellen into closing the inn to everyone but us," he added. Ellen Deavers owned the place and rarely had visitors anyway since Mercy Ridge wasn't exactly a hotbed for tourism. "We can get the adjoining rooms on the second floor, and one of the other deputies can sleep downstairs."

"That might work," Kara said after releasing her bottom lip that she'd been biting. "We'd still have to keep Sadie away from the windows."

"Noreen and you, too," he emphasized. "I don't want either of you taking any unnecessary risks."

Especially since the necessary ones were plentiful enough. After all, Daniel would have to take them out in the open to get them from his ranch to the inn.

"You're okay with connecting rooms?" Kara asked.

Daniel couldn't pretend that he didn't know exactly what she meant. This was about the heat that was still in full simmer mode. Being under the same roof with Kara could send it from simmer to boil. But again, it was a risk he had to take. No way did he want her out of his sight as long as she was in the crosshairs of a killer.

"I'm okay with it," he said.

Again, their gazes held, and it seemed as if she were trying to figure out if that were true. However, she didn't get a chance to do that because his phone rang, and when Kara saw

Barrett's name on the screen, it got her attention. It got Daniel's, too, because this was almost certainly connected to the investigation. He hit the answer button and put it on speaker so that Kara could hear.

"I've got bad news," Barrett immediately said. His brother didn't wait for them to verbally respond to that, but inside, Daniel felt the punch of dread. A moment later, the dread was confirmed when Barrett added, "There's been another murder."

Chapter Five

Loretta Eaton, the office manager at the fertility clinic, was dead.

That was the thought that had run through Kara's head most of the night, and it was one of the reasons she hadn't gotten much sleep. Of course, it hadn't helped that she'd spent the night in a bathtub and knew that Sadie had done the same. Kara hated that such measures had been needed to keep the girl safe. Hated even more that such measures would have to continue, well, indefinitely.

From what Daniel and she had learned, Loretta had gone into the office to check the files on Mandy and according to the San Antonio cops, the woman hadn't made it out of the building alive. When Kara had finally gone off to "bed," they hadn't yet received a time of death from the medical examiner, but according to the security login, Loretta had been in the fertility clinic about two hours before her lifeless body was discovered by a janitor.

Kara hadn't needed any further proof that all these deaths were connected to Willingham Fertility Clinic, but Loretta's murder added to the weight of the case. There were now three confirmed deaths: Mandy Vera, Loretta Eaton and Brenda McGill. Marissa Rucker was still missing, and Kara could only pray that she was still alive and would stay that way. If Marissa had figured out what was going on, that her life was in danger, maybe she went into hiding. At the moment, that was the best possible scenario when it came to Kara's fellow surrogate.

Kara finished her shower and dressed in jeans and a top, and she used some makeup that one of Daniel's ranch hands had brought over from her place. Whoever had processed her house for evidence must have cleared the items since they'd been waiting for her when she got up.

She tried her best to hide the dark circles under her eyes. Even though Sadie probably wouldn't notice something like that, Kara didn't want to give the little girl any reason for concern. Ditto for Daniel. He was already worried about a killer and didn't need to spare any of his thoughts to her well-being.

Following the smell of coffee and the sound of Sadie's babblings, Kara made her way to the kitchen. Everyone was already up, making her feel a little like a slacker. Sadie was in her highchair eating bits of scrambled egg and cut-up fruit. Noreen was at the stove, and Daniel was at the table, sipping coffee while he read something on his laptop.

Noreen was wearing one of her usual loose cotton dresses and white sneakers, and she gave Kara a quick smile that didn't quite make it to her weathered blue eyes. Since Noreen was a local, Kara had known the woman her entire life, and she was as steady as they came, having raised her three now grown sons on her own after her husband had been killed when the boys were children. That steadiness would come in handy with what they were facing.

Daniel glanced up at her, studying her face, and her frown. Obviously, her makeup attempt hadn't fooled him one bit. She must have looked as exhausted as she was.

"Nantie," Sadie greeted, which was her attempt at *Auntie*. Thankfully, she was grinning and showed no signs of stress.

"Good morning, sweetheart," Kara murmured, giving Sadie a kiss. Her dark curls were haloing around her pretty face, and her gray eyes practically sparkled.

Sadie added a hug to the kiss, her sticky fingers leaving bits of egg and strawberry in Kara's hair. She didn't mind. Despite the horrible circumstances, it felt good to see her niece first thing in the morning. It was a rare treat that would help her get through this.

"Have some coffee," Noreen offered, and she stopped scrambling more eggs to get Kara a mug.

Kara filled the mug to the brim, certain that she would need lots of caffeine to make it through the day, and she turned back to Daniel to ask if there were any updates. However, before she could say a word, his phone rang.

"Barrett," he mumbled, already standing. "I need to take this." He answered it while walking out of the room. Obviously, he was worried about Sadie overhearing something she shouldn't.

Noreen sighed, shook her head. "Daniel's worried sick," she whispered. "So are you."

Kara didn't deny it. Couldn't. "How about you?" she asked the nanny. "How are you holding up?"

"About as well as can be expected," she said,

still whispering. "I'm trying to stay calm for Sadie's sake."

Kara was trying to do the same. "Did Daniel talk to you about all of us staying at the inn?"

She nodded, dished up the scrambled eggs that she then handed to Kara. "I've already gotten Sadie's things together. Eat," she added, stepping away from her to load the dishwasher.

Kara wasn't hungry. In fact, her stomach was in knots, but she had to eat. She wouldn't be any good to Daniel and this investigation if she walked around with a light head.

She ate standing, her back against the counter and her gaze on the living room where Daniel was talking on the phone and pacing. Whatever Barrett was telling him had caused Daniel's forehead to bunch up.

"You're worried about him," Noreen said, startling Kara and causing her to practically snap toward the woman.

There'd been something in Noreen's tone. Something that went beyond concern for their safety. That same something was in the woman's eyes, and it made Kara believe that maybe Noreen had picked up on the attraction between Daniel and her.

Noreen managed a slight smile. "I always figured Daniel and you would get together."

It was a good thing that Kara had already swallowed the coffee and eggs, or she would have choked. "It's not like that between Daniel and me," she assured the woman.

Noreen shrugged in a "suit yourself" gesture. "I think it's what your sister would have wanted, too."

Kara didn't even want to consider that. She didn't want that idea in her head. But it was too late. It was already there. It had been for months now. Before Maryanne died, Daniel had been her sister's husband. Period. Of course, Kara had noticed he was hot. She would have been blind not to see that, but he'd been hands-off. Now, her body was nudging her to test that hands-off rule.

And that could be a huge mistake.

If Daniel and she did try for a relationship, and it failed, Sadie could end up being hurt. Kara didn't want any awkwardness between Daniel and her. It just wasn't worth the risk.

She mentally repeated that to herself. Twice.

But, oh, her body could spin some images. Unfortunately, those images were fueled by actual memories of the time she'd seen him and his brothers skinny-dipping in the creek. Even then, he'd been Maryanne's, but that hadn't stopped the memory of him, naked, lean and amazing, from being branded in her mind.

"Let me get Sadie cleaned up while Daniel and you talk," Noreen said.

It took Kara a moment to pull herself out of her heated daydream and realize that Daniel had ended his call with Barrett and was making his way back into the kitchen. One look at his somber face and Kara knew this was a conversation that Sadie definitely shouldn't overhear.

Sadie insisted on giving her daddy a sticky kiss and hug before Noreen whisked her away. It didn't take long, but during that handful of seconds, Kara could feel the anxiety build inside her.

"Has there been another murder?" she came out and asked.

"No." He dragged in a long breath. "Barrett got an update from the ME about Loretta. She died from blunt force trauma. Multiple blows to the head," Daniel added in a mumble. "Barrett saw the crime scene photos, and he said there was a lot of rage in the attack. Plenty of overkill."

That turned her anxiety to an ice-cold chill. Kara could almost see Loretta's beaten body, could feel the terror the woman had gone through before some monster ended her life.

"Are we dealing with two attackers?" Kara asked, forcing her mind back on the investigation. The only way she could help Loretta now was to find her killer and get justice.

"Maybe, but there was over an hour between the attack on us and Lorctta's estimated time of death. That's plenty enough time for our attacker to make it to the clinic." Daniel paused. "San Antonio PD found several tiny cameras planted throughout the clinic. Ones that didn't belong to the clinic's security system."

Kara took a moment to process that. "The cops believe whoever planted the cameras knew that Loretta was there and went after her?"

He nodded. "The question is why. Loretta had already confirmed that Mandy Vera was a surrogate, but she'd also searched some other files. We don't have the details on that yet, but we should soon." Daniel checked the time. "Someone from the clinic should be calling me any minute now."

Good. Maybe that person would be able to tell them what Loretta had been searching. It had to be more than simply providing them info about Mandy since Daniel would have gotten that intel shortly after he verified who she was. Of course, maybe the killer just wanted Loretta dead so that she couldn't give them anything that would help the cops catch him.

Overkill and caution.

Take out a potential threat before it became a real threat.

Of course, when the cops continued to dig, they might discover that Loretta had some kind of connection to the killer. Maybe even be an accomplice. But if that were true, it didn't seem as if the woman would have been so quick to cooperate with them by confirming the info she'd given them on Mandy.

"San Antonio PD is giving me access to the files of the murdered surrogates and the missing one," Daniel continued. "They're not dismissing the theory that Brenda was killed by her abusive boyfriend, but in light of everything else, they're going to treat her murder as connected to the others."

"Good," Kara murmured, and she felt the knotted tension inside her ease up a little. "Maybe there's something from the crime scene that can help ID the person."

Daniel nodded and stared at her as if he wanted to say more. More that might not be connected to the murders. He finally huffed and groaned softly. "I don't want this thing between us to get out of hand."

Kara definitely didn't ask him to clarify what *thing*. She knew. And she just happened to agree with him. Unfortunately, she wasn't sure their feelings for each other were in their control. It was hard to turn off the heat when you didn't know how or when your body kept urging you to do something about it. Still, she made a sound of agreement and hoped that being under the same roof with Daniel wouldn't break down the defenses she was trying to build to contain this heat.

As if relieved over the interruption, Daniel immediately took out his phone when it rang. "It's the fertility clinic," he relayed to her, and he hit the speaker function as he answered, "Deputy Logan from Mercy Ridge."

"Hello," the woman said, and that one-word greeting seemed very shaky. Of course, with a murder inside the clinic, Kara suspected that tensions and fear were running high. "I'm Betty Hyde. I was Loretta's assistant, and I'll be taking over her duties until they can hire someone else."

The woman's voice not only cracked but Kara could hear her breath break into a sob.

"You were close to Loretta?" Daniel asked.

"No. Not really. But... God, she's dead. Someone killed her."

"I know. I'm sorry." In contrast, Daniel kept his voice level and calm. "I know this is a hard time for you and everyone else there, but I'm hoping you can help."

"Yes," Betty muttered. "The other cops told me that you needed copies of any threatening letters and emails we've received in the last year. I've got those for you. Well, I have the letters, including the one from the person who claimed to have killed Brenda McGill, but someone hacked into our computer files about two months ago and deleted a lot of stuff. Including the email threats."

Daniel and she exchanged a knowing glance. Kara seriously doubted that was a coincidence. One of those deleted threats would have likely pointed to the killer.

"There are two letters in particular that caught my attention," Betty went on a moment later. "The first is the one that mentioned Brenda. There's no name, no signature and the crime lab wasn't able to find any DNA on it. The police still have the original, but there's a copy here in our files."

Kara hadn't known the letter had been

tested, but she was glad the San Antonio cops were taking those kinds of measures. Too bad the person who'd written it hadn't left behind any kind of trace evidence.

"And the other letter that caught your attention?" Daniel prompted.

"There's no signature or return address on it, either," Betty explained. "I can send you a copy of it."

"Do that," Daniel insisted, giving the woman his email address. "In the meantime, give me the gist of the letter."

"The person threatened the clinic," Betty said without hesitation. "Other clinics in the city were threatened as well, and the same language was used in each one. Using a lot of profanity, he said he was going to make everyone pay, that we'd all be sorry for turning innocent young girls into surrogates."

"He?" Daniel questioned. "You're sure the person who wrote it was a man?"

"Yes. Well, I'm sure if he's telling the truth. He claims to have had a daughter who was talked into becoming a surrogate, and she died."

Kara immediately got a flash of a memory. When Maryanne and she had been researching the clinic, Kara had read something about a surrogate dying shortly after giving birth.

"Do you know the name of the surrogate who died?" Kara asked. Then she remembered that she hadn't introduced herself so Betty wouldn't have any idea who she was. "I'm Kara Holland. I was a surrogate at Willingham, and last night someone tried to kill me."

Kara heard the woman's sharp intake of breath. "So, you think this is connected to what happened to Loretta?"

"I do. Do you keep records on the surrogates after they deliver?" Kara pressed.

"No, I'm sorry. The surrogates or the biological parents choose the facility and hospital where they want to receive medical care."

That had been true in Kara's case. She'd chosen to give birth in Mercy Ridge, and she'd had no follow-up with Willingham Clinic after Sadie's birth. Still, she pushed.

"I remember hearing about a surrogate who died," Kara said. "This would have been well over two years ago. I seem to recall she died from a blood clot a few days after she delivered."

"I'm sorry," Betty repeated. "I don't know anything..." Then she paused. "Wait. I do recall something like that." Kara heard the click of keys on a computer keyboard. "I wasn't working here then, but I heard someone mention it."

Obviously, Betty was searching for a name. Something that Kara was also doing. She remembered coming across the woman's name during her research. It had been an awful tragedy, but Kara hadn't put the blame for her death on the clinic.

"Clarice Stroud," Betty blurted out. "She was a surrogate here, but she died at a hospital in Austin."

Bingo. That was the same name Kara had seen, and she looked up at Daniel to see if he thought it might be an important connection. He did.

"I'll want a copy of that second letter," Daniel reminded the woman, "and I'll contact SAPD to have them pick up the original. I want them to have another look at it and send it to the lab."

"Of course," Betty agreed. "I'll get that copy to you right away."

"One more thing," Daniel said. "Could you give me the next-of-kin contact for Clarice Stroud? It's important," he added when she made a sound to indicate that might be a problem. "This could end up saving another woman's life."

"Oh, God," Betty muttered, and after a few seconds, Kara heard more clicks on the keyboard. "Clarice only had one next of kin listed. Her father, Eldon Stroud. He lives on a ranch about thirty miles from where you are. Mercy Ridge."

Daniel jotted down the address Betty gave him, and the moment he ended the call, he made another one. To Barrett.

"We've got a possible person of interest in the murders," Daniel immediately told his brother. "I need you to get Eldon Stroud in ASAP for questioning."

Chapter Six

Daniel read through the copy of the letter that Betty had just emailed him. The woman had been right about the profanity and the threats. The venom was practically coming off the words in dangerous, heated waves, but Daniel zoomed right in on one particular sentence.

Somebody will pay for what happened to my girl.

Daniel didn't know the background of why Clarice Stroud had become a surrogate, not yet anyway, but if this letter was truly her father's rantings, then he obviously believed his daughter had been pressured into going through with a pregnancy. A pregnancy that had perhaps contributed to her death.

That caused Daniel to stop, and he cursed while he pressed in Barrett's number again.

"What's wrong?" Kara asked. She was

shoulder to shoulder with him as they sat at the kitchen table reading the letter on his laptop.

"Whoever hired Clarice could be in danger," he managed to explain right before Barrett answered. He ignored Kara's gasp and told his brother what was going on. "Eldon's daughter, Clarice, was a surrogate who died shortly after giving birth. We need a court order to find out whose baby she carried."

"I'll get on that," Barrett assured him. "I'm still trying to get in touch with Eldon. He's not answering his phone so I'm going to send a deputy out to his place."

Good. Daniel wished he could be the one to go out and face down this man, but he couldn't leave just yet. Not until he had Noreen, Sadie and Kara moved into the inn where they'd hopefully be safer than they were here at his ranch.

"Go ahead and send Leo out here with a cruiser," Daniel added to his brother.

He didn't want to drive them to the inn in his SUV in case of another attack. The cruiser was bullet resistant, something that he prayed they wouldn't need. Still, he wanted to take the precaution.

When he got Barrett's assurance that he'd take care of sending the cruiser, Daniel stood to check on Noreen and see if she was about ready to go, but the sound of an approaching vehicle stopped him. It was barely eight in the morning, and he wasn't expecting any visitors.

"Stay back," he warned Kara.

With the attack from the night before still way too fresh in his mind, he drew his gun and went to the front of the house to look out the window. The person he saw caused him to mutter some profanity.

"Who is it?" Kara asked. He could hear the real question in her fear-laced voice. *Is it the killer?*

"It's Neal Rizzo," he spat out.

There was no need for him to explain to her who that was. Mercy Ridge was a small town where everybody knew everyone else's business. That meant there wasn't anybody over the age of five who hadn't heard about Daniel's run-ins with Neal Rizzo, his neighbor who liked to stir up trouble. If there was a beef to find, Rizzo would locate it and try to make it worse.

That was especially true after their last run-in.

A couple of months ago, Daniel had gotten an anonymous tip that Rizzo was a member of a militia group that might be stockpiling weapons, and Daniel had gone over to Rizzo's ranch to have a chat with him. He hadn't arrested Rizzo. Hadn't gotten in his face. *Too much*. But he had made it clear to Rizzo that if he was involved in any illegal activity, he'd uncover it and arrest him.

Rizzo hadn't taken that well.

Judging from the tight muscles in his face when he stepped from his truck, the man still wasn't taking it well.

"Stay back," Daniel repeated to Kara.

He disengaged the security system so he could open the door. Daniel stepped onto the porch, and as expected, that stopped Rizzo from coming closer. He doubted that Rizzo would do something stupid like open fire—especially considering that two of Daniel's ranch hands were watching—but after the attack from the night before, he wasn't taking any chances. He didn't want Rizzo any closer to his house than he already was.

Rizzo had brought his own ranch hands, and while they stayed in the truck, Daniel thought they looked more like hired thugs than cowboys. Maybe they were part of the militia group. If so, it was stupid for Rizzo to bring them here and try to rub it in Daniel's face.

"Some of your livestock broke fence and got onto my property," Rizzo snarled.

Daniel looked at his ranch hand Tanner Parnell to see if he knew anything about it. Tanner nodded. "It happened about an hour ago, and I was coming to tell you." Tanner shot Rizzo a narrow-eyed glance. "But it doesn't look as if the livestock tore down the fence. My guess is that someone did it."

Tanner gave Rizzo another of those glances, probably to emphasize that he believed Rizzo or one of his men were responsible. Daniel wouldn't put it past Rizzo to give an order like that.

"I'll send you a bill because your livestock tore up some of my pasture," Rizzo went on. "The next time it happens, something bad could happen to them. Maybe my men will mistake them for deer and shoot them."

"Then your men are dumber than dirt if they can't tell the difference between an Angus and a deer. But just in case they are that stupid, you should probably know that the laws have tightened up on that sort of thing. The legal thing to do is inform me that my livestock are on your property and give me a chance to remove them."

That sure didn't help the tight muscles in

Rizzo's jaw. Every inch of him vibrated with insult and anger.

"And FYI, if you did shoot my cattle," Daniel went on, "I'd have to examine the fence that you say they broke. Outside authorities would be called in to help with the investigation. It'd be interesting to find out if there's any trace evidence or DNA that would ID the person responsible. That could result in all sorts of charges like destruction of property and cattle rustling."

Daniel hadn't known for sure that Rizzo or his men had indeed cut that fence, but he knew it now. Rizzo confirmed it with the stone-cold glower he aimed at Daniel. The man certainly didn't jump to deny that he'd done such a thing or that he'd ordered it to be done.

"This isn't over," Rizzo spat out. "You're not just going to stick your nose in my business and get away with it."

Daniel tapped his badge. "Your business is mine when you're suspected of doing something illegal. The investigation into your involvement in the militia is open and ongoing. Cutting my fence isn't going to make me step back on that."

That kicked the man's anger up even higher.

"You deserve to go down," Rizzo threatened. "You deserve to burn in hell."

With that, Rizzo turned and stalked back to his truck. With his hand on the butt of his weapon, Daniel stood there and watched as he sped away. Even though Rizzo was gone, his rage still hung in the air like a dark and dangerous cloud.

"You think we should set up cameras out in the pastures?" Tanner asked.

It was something Daniel had already considered. Not because of Rizzo. But in case the threats from the killer continued. After all, he couldn't stay at the inn indefinitely, and he'd have to beef up security in order to be able to live here with Sadie.

"Arrange for the cameras," Daniel instructed Tanner, and the hand took out his phone, no doubt to get that started.

But Daniel continued to stand there. Thinking. Remembering that look on Rizzo's face. The anger in his threat.

And he had to consider something.

The timing of this fence incident was maybe not a coincidence. News of the attack had to be all over Mercy Ridge, so maybe Rizzo wanted to add to the troubles. Or worse.

Maybe Rizzo was the cause of them.

Even though it was probably a long stretch, Daniel went back to something that Betty had said. The fertility clinic's records had been hacked into two months ago. That was around the same time that Daniel had confronted Rizzo about his ties to the militia. Rizzo knew full well that Kara, Maryanne and he had used that clinic to have Sadie, so maybe…

Hell.

Was that possible?

Had Rizzo set some kind of sick plan in motion? One with an ultimate goal to stop him from digging further into the militia investigation?

"What's wrong?" he heard Kara ask.

He glanced over his shoulder to see her in the foyer. A new wave of worry was in her eyes.

"You heard what Rizzo said?" Daniel asked, going back in. He moved her away from the door so he could shut it and reset the security system.

Kara nodded and studied his face as if trying to figure out what was going on in his head. He doubted she would believe his theory, but he laid it out for her, anyway.

"Rizzo's bad news," he said. "I haven't been

able to prove it, but he's connected to a militia that's involved in illegal arms sales."

Daniel paused only so he could figure out the best way to word the rest of what he was about to tell her, but Kara spoke before he could say anything else.

"You believe he's involved with the surrogate murders and last night's attack on us?" she asked.

Believe was a strong word. Right now, it was just something that had started to take root, and it could end up causing him to take a wrong turn with the investigation. "Rizzo's got motive to want to get back at me, but he's not stupid. He has to know if something happens to me now that he'd be a prime suspect."

Kara nodded. "But if Rizzo used the fertility clinic as a cover, then your death could be pinned on the surrogate killer."

He was glad she'd reached the same conclusion he had. Yes, it was possible that Rizzo was behind this.

Possible.

But a stronger suspect was Eldon Stroud. Daniel needed to question the man ASAP, but he'd also do some checking to see if there was anything to connect Rizzo to the murders. Unfortunately, with those militia ties, Rizzo wouldn't have necessarily had to hire a killer because he could have had one of his fellow militia cohorts do the deed. If that'd happened, there wouldn't be a money trail. Still, people talked, and it wasn't easy to keep multiple murders and attempted murders a secret.

When Kara grew quiet, Daniel looked at her. Yeah, the fear was back, and he doubted it was all for her. The baby she'd carried and loved was caught up in the middle of this. And he might be the reason for the danger.

Daniel silently cursed.

"This isn't your fault," Kara murmured as if she'd known exactly what he was thinking. She touched his arm, gave it a gentle rub with just two of her fingers. "Even if it's Rizzo who's behind all of this, this isn't your fault," she emphasized.

He wasn't sure he could believe that, and it didn't matter that he'd been doing his job when he'd questioned Rizzo. None of that mattered if the SOB went after anyone else.

Once again, he found himself staring into Kara's eyes. The fear was easing some. Not the worry, though. He figured that was here to stay until they solved this case and got on with their lives. He only hoped that was possible. But it seemed each time he looked at Kara this way, it was sending him further down a very tricky path. One that he knew wasn't smart to go down. Even after the danger ended, maybe there was no turning back from that. Maybe things had already changed and they'd never be able to go back to the way things were.

Daniel welcomed the distraction of his phonc ringing. Best not to stand around staring into Kara's eyes. Especially when it was Leo's name on the screen.

"I'm nearly at your place," Leo said when Daniel answered.

"Tell Noreen we're ready to go," Daniel instructed Kara, and he waited for her to leave before he continued with his brother. "By any chance, did you see Rizzo on the road leading here?"

"No." Leo paused. "Why? Is he giving you trouble again?"

"Trying to. I want to see if I can connect him to anything at the fertility clinic or the murders."

"All right," his brother said without missing a beat. "I can help with that. Maybe SAPD can give us something, too. By the way, a couple of the homicide detectives there agreed to contact anyone who's been a surrogate at the clinic for the past two years. They'll warn them of the possible danger and offer protection to any one of them who wants it."

Good. That'd perhaps take a lot of manpower, but it might prevent someone else from being killed.

"I'm pulling up in front of your house now," Leo added.

Daniel did indeed hear the cruiser's engine, and he checked out the window to make sure it was his brother. It was. "We'll be out in a few," he told Leo and ended the call.

He turned to get Noreen, Sadie and Kara, but they were already heading his way. With a diaper bag looped over her shoulder, Noreen was carrying Sadie, and Kara had their suitcases, one in each hand. Daniel wouldn't be able to help her with that because he wanted to be able to draw his weapon if necessary. He hoped like the devil that it wouldn't be necessary, though.

"We move fast," Daniel told them and was thankful that Sadie was smiling as if this was some sort of fun game. "The three of you will go in the back seat. I'll ride shotgun."

Noreen gave a shaky nod. She was afraid but as determined as he was to make this trip fast and safe. Kara's sound of agreement wasn't shaky at all. He could see a steely resolve in her expression. Good. Because he needed everyone to be ready to protect Sadie.

At the knock on the door, Daniel disengaged the security system so he could open the door to let Leo in. His brother kept things light, too, giving Sadie a quick kiss before they hurried out together.

Daniel and Leo stayed on the sides of Noreen and Kara. Using their bodies to shield them. It wouldn't stop a sniper, but if someone had been in place to shoot, Daniel figured those shots would have happened when he'd been talking to Rizzo. Of course, that only applied if he was the target. If it was Kara the killer wanted, then this could turn deadly fast.

He fired his gaze all around the yard and ranch, and the second they all reached the cruiser, Daniel practically shoved Kara and Noreen inside it. His brother had thought to put in a car seat, which looked out of place in the center back of a cruiser, but Daniel was thankful for it. Thankful, too, when he had everyone inside the bullet-resistant vehicle.

Daniel could finally release the breath he'd been holding. No way, though, would his heartrate ease up until he had them safely at the inn. That would be another breath-holding situation, but at least Leo would be able to pull right up to the back porch of the inn. It would still mean they'd be out in the open, but there'd be fewer places for a gunman to hide there. Added to that, Barrett had already sent out reserve deputies to patrol the grounds of the inn.

As soon as Noreen had Sadie in the car seat, Leo took off.

Kara had to adjust the suitcases, which thankfully weren't full-sized, and she stacked them on her lap. It wouldn't make it easy for her to get down on the seat if it came to that, but he hadn't wanted to risk taking the time to put them in the trunk.

"Ites," Sadie blurted out, clapping her hands.

"Lights," Daniel translated for Leo.

About a month earlier, Barrett had dropped by the ranch in the cruiser, and he'd shown Sadie the blue emergency lights. Obviously, they'd made an impression on his little girl.

Leo turned on the lights, including the one on the dash. It was actually the only one that Sadie could see from inside the car, but again, it made an impression. She squealed with delight, and despite their circumstances, it made everyone else in the cruiser smile.

Leo kept the lights on as he drove away from the ranch, and even though a cruiser with whirling lights wouldn't be a deterrent to a killer, it probably wouldn't hurt, either. After all, if the killer had the ranch under surveillance, then he had almost certainly seen Leo arrive.

Not exactly a comforting thought.

Daniel continued to keep watch as they made their way to the road that would lead them to town. Leo was doing the same. He saw that Kara was, too, after he glanced in the mirror. He only looked at her for a split second because something else grabbed his attention.

Leo must have seen it, too, because he hit the brakes, stopping only about twenty-five feet from the turn to the road that led into town.

"What the heck?" Leo muttered, and both Daniel and he drew their guns.

There was a person, a woman, lying on the ground just ahead of them. She wasn't moving but was instead stretched out on her back, her arms and legs forming an *x*. And Daniel had no trouble seeing what was on her light-colored clothes.

Blood.

Chapter Seven

Kara's heart went to her knees. She got just a glimpse of the bloody woman lying on the road before she threw her hand in front of Sadie to shelter her eyes.

Thankfully, the little girl wasn't paying any attention to what was beyond the whirling blue emergency lights, but just in case, Kara directed Sadie's attention to her phone that she pulled from her pocket. Kara loaded a cute kitten video and handed it to Sadie for her to watch.

"Is she alive?" Kara asked, trying to choose her words carefully. She hadn't wanted to say *dead*, though that certainly seemed to be the case.

Oh, God.

Had another woman been murdered?

"It could be a trap," Daniel muttered just loud enough for her to hear.

That gave Kara a jolt of adrenaline. Her gaze flew around, looking for any signs of danger. From the front seat, Leo and Daniel were doing the same. Leo called in the incident to Dispatch, reporting the location of the body. Or maybe not a body at all but rather a person who was pretending to be dead. Either way, Leo requested an ambulance and backup.

"Drive around the woman," Daniel instructed his brother. "Don't stop. The EMTs will take care of her when they get here."

Kara knew that had to be hard for Daniel, especially if the woman truly did need help, but getting out to check on her could result in the killer launching a full-scale attack on them. Sadie could be hurt. Or worse.

Leo inched the cruiser forward, maneuvering around the road so that the woman was on the passenger's side of the cruiser. There wasn't room for him to get around her any other way. That gave both Daniel and Kara the chance to get a good look at her.

Even though her voice and hands were shaking, Noreen managed to keep Sadie's attention on the kitten video. Kara, however, looked down at the ground as they drove past the woman. She definitely looked dead, and it was either an excellent makeup job or else there truly was a gaping hole in her chest.

Seeing all the blood turned her stomach, but Kara forced herself to look at the woman's face.

And she bit back the profanity that came with the shock.

"I know her," Kara blurted out, and she would have bolted from the cruiser to try to help if Daniel hadn't reached over the seat and taken hold of her.

"Stay put," he warned her. And much to her horror, he opened his cruiser door while barking out to Leo, "Cover me."

Leo probably would have cursed had Sadie not been there, but he did cover his brother as Daniel opened his door and leaned out enough so he could reach the woman. It took some doing, and he was obviously trying to stay behind the cover of the door, but he touched his fingers to her neck. He didn't say anything, but the look he gave Kara confirmed it.

The woman was dead.

This wasn't some ruse. Well, not on her part. That didn't mean her killer wasn't nearby, waiting for a chance to kill them. That was no doubt why Daniel didn't waste any time closing his door, and the second he did that, Leo sped away.

"Who is she?" Daniel asked.

Kara's heart was beating so loud, the sound pounding in her ears, that it took her a moment to realize what he'd said. "She's Georgia," Kara managed to tell him. "I can't remember her last namc, but..." She had to stop and swallow hard before she could continue. "I met her at the fertility clinic when we were both waiting for appointments. She was a surrogate."

And just saying that filled her with a new wave of dread. Another connection to Willingham Fertility Clinic. Another dead surrogate.

Her breath broke, and she couldn't stop the hoarse groan that tore from her mouth. Sadie clearly thought this was a game because she giggled and tried to imitate it before Noreen got the child's attention back on the video.

"Obviously, the body wasn't there when I drove by less than ten minutes ago," Leo murmured. The moment he was on the highway, he hit the accelerator to get them out of there.

Ten minutes. That wasn't much time, but Kara had no idea how much time it would take to drag a body from a vehicle or the ditch and pose it that way. It was possible Georgia had been dead for hours. Days even. Of course, it was just as possible the woman had been murdered in the short time that Leo was at Daniel's ranch.

Kara tried to tamp down the swell of emotions. Definitely tried to make sure she kept the stark expression off her face so that Sadie wouldn't see it and get upset.

She fired glances all around, keeping watch. Staying alert. There were no signs of the killer, but Kara's thoughts immediately went to Rizzo. This could still be connected to him. After all, the man had just been at the ranch, and while he wouldn't be able to see Daniel's ranch from his place, he could have been watching the road.

Daniel took out his phone, and Kara saw him press Barrett's number. "I need to give Barrett an update about this," he said. However, he didn't put the call on speaker. Again, probably because of Sadie.

"The DB is a female, midtwenties. About five-six, medium build. Brown hair and eyes," Daniel told his brother when he answered. "COD appears to be gunshot wound to the chest." He whispered that last part. "Kara believes the woman is Georgia, surname unknown, and that she was a surrogate at the fertility clinic around the same time Kara was a patient there."

Daniel had managed to deliver all of that info in his cop voice. It was void of emotion, but Kara knew there was no such void inside him. He was almost certainly feeling plenty of anger and disgust, coupled with the need to put a stop to this now. Too many people had already died, and they weren't even close to being able to find the killer and put an end to the danger.

"Georgia Marshall," Daniel said a moment later, obviously repeating what Barrett had told him. Barrett must have already had access to the files from the clinic to be able to pull it up that fast.

Daniel looked back at her to see if she could confirm that, but Kara had to shake her head. "I only met her once, and I'm not sure we even exchanged surnames."

The only reason Kara remembered Georgia was because the woman had made a comment along the lines of her name being the same as the state where her mother had been born.

Daniel gave her a nod, relayed that to his brother and then said, "Eldon Stroud. Did you get in touch with him?"

Kara couldn't hear Barrett's response, but

a moment later, Daniel added, "Good. I'll be interested in hearing if he has an alibi for last night and this morning."

Hearing that helped the tightening in Kara's chest to ease up some. Maybe Eldon could give them some answers. Heck, maybe he'd just confess to everything so that Barrett could lock him up.

"Stroud is coming in for an interview this afternoon," Daniel relayed to Kara in a whisper.

"Rizzo showed up at my place this morning," Daniel went on, talking to his brother now. "He's like a pressure cooker about to go off." It seemed as if he was about to say more, but his gaze drifted back to Sadie. She was no longer watching the video, and Noreen couldn't seem to get her attention off Daniel. "Bring in Rizzo for an interview," he finally said to Barrett. "See if you can convince him to be tested for gunshot residue."

That was a good call if Rizzo would agree to something like that. Kara doubted that he would even if he was innocent. Rizzo didn't seem the sort to cooperate with the law, especially when the sheriff was Daniel's brother.

Daniel ended the call just as Leo pulled to a stop at the rear entrance to the Serenity

Inn. Other than the owner's car, there were no other vehicles in the tiny parking lot. No one in the yard, either, but Daniel, Leo and Kara still glanced around, making sure it was safe to move Sadie.

Even though Kara often drove by the inn, she tried to look at it with a fresh eye. The two-story white Victorian was one of the oldest houses in Mercy Ridge, and the owner, Ellen Deavers, kept it in pristine condition. Flower beds burst with color, and while there was no fence, low-growing manicured hedges marked the property lines.

Kara glanced at the motion-activated lights that would no doubt flare on if someone came into the yard. There'd be a decent security system inside, too. Ellen was friendly. Welcoming, even. But she was also a woman in her sixties who was often alone. She hadn't wanted her beautiful home to be easy pickings for someone out to steal something, so she'd added far more security than most folks had.

Daniel and Leo got out together, each of them opening one of the back doors of the cruiser. Leo helped get Sadie out of her car seat, immediately rushing her up the porch steps and into the inn. Noreen was right behind them. Daniel took one of the suitcases from Kara's lap, but he kept his shooting hand free as they hurried inside.

Ellen was there in the large kitchen waiting for them, and she turned on the security system once they'd shut the door. She also handed Daniel a piece of paper with the code and instructions to control the system.

Despite the tense situation, Ellen had a smile for Sadie. By now, though, Sadie wasn't so cheery. Maybe she was picking up on the dour mood because she started to fuss. Adjusting the diaper bag on her shoulder, Noreen took Sadie from Leo.

"Let me read her a story and try to get her to settle down," Noreen suggested.

Ellen nodded. "You can use any room in the place, but there are two large connecting rooms on the second floor. Daniel said something about a deputy staying, too—"

"Cybil Cassidy," Leo provided. "She'll be here before I leave to go back to work."

Kara knew Cybil. She was a deputy who was working on a criminal justice degree. She was young, probably only twenty-four, but from what she'd heard, Cybil was a good cop. She'd certainly come from good stock since her grandfather had once been the sheriff of Mercy Ridge.

"Cybil can stay in a room on the first floor if that works for you," Ellen said. "Maybe the one near the front door?"

Daniel made a sound of agreement, and when Sadie fussed again, he motioned for Noreen to go ahead and take her upstairs. Both Ellen and Leo went with her, each of them taking a suitcase, and Kara had no doubts that Leo would check every inch of the second floor to make sure it was safe. On the bottom floor, Daniel began to do the same.

Kara followed him as they made their way through the large front parlor, where there was a reception desk. Together, they checked the door and every window to make sure they were locked and armed with the security alarm. They also closed the curtains and blinds. It helped settle her nerves a little, but Kara could see much too clearly the images of Georgia lying dead on the road. Images that would no doubt stay with her for a lifetime.

Oh, mercy.

Why was this happening? Why were so many women being murdered? Maybe the interviews Barrett was going to do would give them some answers, but it still wouldn't undo what had already been done. The killer had already taken and ruined so many lives, and there were no guarantees that this wouldn't just continue.

Daniel whirled around to face her, and that's when Kara realized she hadn't quite tamped down the sound that'd torn from her mouth.

"I'm sorry," she said, waving him off when he went to her. "You've got enough to worry about without having to deal with me."

"I want to deal with you," he assured her. Daniel's voice was barely a whisper, and when he pulled her into his arms, he brushed a kiss on the top of her head. "Trust me when I say that I'll do everything I can to keep you safe."

"Ditto." She pulled back, looked up at him and saw his slight smile. "I've always trusted you." But she wanted to wince when she heard her own words. They sounded, well, intimate. As if she meant more than just his keeping her safe.

And she did.

Kara had indeed always trusted him. That had never been a problem between them. The only problem was how to justify the other things she was feeling for him. The heat. The pull of her heart to him. He'd been her sister's husband. Her brother-in-law. And while Maryanne was alive, Kara would have never let her feelings for Daniel cross any lines.

Never.

However, she certainly felt capable of crossing some lines right now.

It was probably a combination of the danger and the spent adrenaline. And the fact that she'd ended up in his arms again. She wasn't at her strongest right now, and she needed to be. Not to resist Daniel. She was no longer sure that was possible. But she needed to be strong to face whatever the killer had in store for them.

"I should check on Sadie," he murmured, but he didn't move. Neither did Kara. Daniel continued to hold her, and she could feel the conflict going on inside him. The moment ended, though, when his phone rang. "Barrett," he said glancing at the screen.

Daniel stepped back and put the call on speaker. "Are you settled in at the inn?" Barrett asked.

"We're here. How long are you going to be able to spare Cybil?"

"As long as necessary," Barrett assured him.

Because she was still close to Daniel, she could see that relaxed him a little. Kara figured there was also a good chance that Leo would be spending some nights here at the inn. Barrett, though, had his own concerns since his fiancée was pregnant.

"I just got off the phone with SAPD," Barrett continued. "Georgia's roommate reported her missing last night when she didn't come home after working her shift at the hospital. She was a nursing assistant."

"Was?" Daniel said. "You're sure the dead woman's Georgia?"

"Yeah. I'm at the scene now, and I found her driver's license. It was tucked underneath her body, so obviously the killer wanted us to know who she was."

Kara got another flash image of the dead woman. She hadn't seen the license, but she agreed with Barrett. The killer wanted them to know Georgia's identity. Wanted them to know that she'd been a surrogate. That way, the mental torture could start right away. Kara was thinking exactly what he no doubt wanted her to think.

Will I be next?

The killer wanted her scared. Wanted to put her through hell and back. But it fired up the simmering anger inside her. She wanted this SOB caught and punished.

"SAPD's still working on contacting all the surrogates," Barrett added a moment later.

"But at least now we have a task force. Since the murders have happened in more than one jurisdiction, the Texas Rangers are coming in to help."

"Good," Daniel answered just as there was a knock at the front door. He motioned for Kara to move to the side of the living room, and once she had, he went to the window and peered out the edge of the curtain.

"Is something wrong?" Barrett asked when Daniel ground out some profanity.

Daniel's reaction didn't send Kara into a panic. To her, he seemed more riled than worried about a threat. "No," Daniel finally said. "It's just Sean Maynard."

Kara pulled back her shoulders in surprise. Sean was a local rancher, and while he wasn't the absolute last person she'd expected to hear from today, she certainly hadn't been expecting him. Especially not here at the inn.

"Kara?" Sean called out.

Once, Sean and she had been lovers, and for a while she'd thought she was in love with him. However, things had gone downhill fast when she'd agreed to become her sister's surrogate. He'd been totally opposed to it and basically given her an ultimatum. Either him or the surrogacy.

Kara hadn't chosen him.

That'd been well over two years ago, and while things weren't exactly friendly between them, she'd thought that she was no longer on his radar. He certainly hadn't been on hers.

"Kara?" Sean said again, and he followed it with a louder knock.

"I'll call you back," Daniel told his brother right before he ended the call.

He disarmed the security system for the front door and he opened it just a crack. Judging from his defensive stance and the way Daniel slid his hand over his gun, he wasn't taking any chances.

"Is Kara here?" Sean asked. "I need to see her. I need to make sure she's okay."

Kara was certain that her own stance was defensive when she went closer to stand by Daniel's side. Sean's attention immediately shifted to her, but Daniel was firing glances all around the small front yard and the street. He was no doubt looking to make sure this wasn't the start of another attack.

"Are you all right?" Sean blurted out, his words running together. His breathing was way too fast, as if he'd just sprinted there. "I heard someone tried to kill you."

She nodded but was puzzled by his reaction. The reaction of someone who'd expected to find her injured or in immediate danger. Of course, everyone in Mercy Ridge had heard about the attack so maybe the gossips had gotten it wrong and were gabbing that she'd been physically hurt.

"How'd you know we were here?" Daniel snapped.

"I saw her in the cruiser when you pulled into the parking lot of the inn," Sean readily answered.

"I didn't see your truck," Kara pointed out.

Sean tipped his head to Main Street. "I was in the hardware store. I was parked at the back."

Daniel made a show of checking his watch. "We've been at the inn for more than five minutes. It wouldn't have taken you that long to walk here."

The steely tone of Daniel's question caused Sean's shoulders to snap back. "I debated if I should come over or try to call you instead, but I figured a visit would be better. I just had to know if Kara was all right."

She couldn't figure out a reason why he would lie about something like that, but then she wasn't exactly in a trusting mood.

Daniel clearly wasn't about to trust Sean,

either, but Kara didn't want this conversation to continue. With the door open, Daniel could become a sniper's target. Best to give Sean the answer he wanted so he'd be on his way.

"I'm okay," she said to Sean, knowing it wasn't anywhere near the truth. However, she didn't want to get into a discussion about her well-being with her ex. Especially when her ex was tossing a few glares at Daniel.

"She's fine," Daniel snapped, and he moved as if to shut the door in Sean's face. But Sean's foot stopped him.

"I'm also here to talk to you," Sean insisted. "Both of you," he amended. "I have some information about the murdered surrogates."

Chapter Eight

Until Sean had said that last part—*I have some information about the murdered surrogates*—Daniel had been about to slam the door in the man's face. But hearing that sure stopped him.

"Information?" Daniel repeated, and he didn't bother to take the skepticism out of his tone or the glare he was aiming at Kara's ex.

Being her ex didn't have anything to do with his extreme dislike of the man, Daniel assured himself. No. This had nothing to do with the attraction simmering between Kara and him, and it wasn't the reason Daniel's glare intensified. He had other reasons for despising Sean. The man had treated Kara like dirt after she'd told him about the surrogacy.

"Information," Sean verified, keeping his gaze focused on Kara. "This morning when I checked the mail, there was a letter. Whoever wrote it said you were in danger and that Daniel's responsible."

Well, that got Daniel's attention. Kara's, too, because she moved even closer to Daniel, maybe so he could meet Sean's gaze head-on. However, in doing that, she also put herself in a possible line of fire. That's why Daniel stepped back, and he motioned for Sean to follow them into the foyer. Daniel also kept his gun ready in case this turned out to be some kind of dangerous ruse.

He'd never thought of Sean as a potential killer, but there was a whole lot of anger simmering beneath the surface. People with that kind of anger could snap.

Had that happened to Sean?

Daniel had to look at it from that angle. Sean was bitter over his breakup with Kara so maybe he could have orchestrated a way to murder both of them to get his revenge. That was a long shot, but Daniel intended to be cautious enough not to overlook anything. Including that Sean might try to attack them now. And that's why he moved Kara behind him.

Sean noticed the maneuver, and it caused him to turn a scowl on Daniel. Daniel scowled right back at him, and he was certain he could pull off that particular expression better than

Sean. The stakes weren't nearly as high for Sean as they were for Kara and him.

"Leo, stay upstairs with the others," Daniel called out to his brother. He definitely didn't want Noreen bringing Sadie down right now.

"Is there trouble?" Leo immediately asked.

"To be determined." He kept his glare on Sean. "Tell me about this letter you say you got."

Sean definitely didn't blurt out any info. Instead, he shifted his gaze back to Kara, and Daniel didn't think it was his imagination that Sean was waiting to see if she'd jump to his defense.

She didn't.

That didn't improve Sean's mood, but it should have been what he expected. Kara and he weren't exactly on friendly terms, and women were dying. Anyone who'd had a past grudge with Daniel or her was suspect.

"The letter is in my pocket," Sean finally snarled to Daniel. "Don't shoot me when I take it out."

"Then make sure you don't take out a gun with it," Daniel fired back.

"I didn't have to come here, you know," Sean grumbled, pulling the bent envelope from his back jeans pocket.

Daniel watched the man's every move. "You did if you actually have relevant information about an ongoing murder investigation. That's the law."

The man's glare stayed locked with his, but Sean gave the envelope to Kara. Daniel didn't mind that because he wanted his own hands free in case he had to do something to restrain, or stop, Sean.

Sean's name was typed on the envelope, but there was no return address. The postmark was from San Antonio and had been sent two days ago. It normally only took a day to get mail from San Antonio, but it was possible that it'd been delivered yesterday and that Sean had just now found it.

Possible.

"Should I read it?" she asked Daniel. "Will I contaminate it?"

Yeah, she could indeed contaminate it. If it was actual evidence, that is. That fell into the "to be determined" category, too. Still, the envelope had clearly been handled and opened so any trace or prints that might be there had already been compromised. Added to that, he couldn't send it to the crime lab until he believed this might actually pertain to the case.

"Read it," Daniel instructed.

Making glances from the corner of his eye, Daniel saw Kara slide the letter from the envelope. It was a single page with a few lines of typewritten words.

"'Sean,'" Kara said, reading it aloud. "'If you still care for Kara Holland, you'll get her away from Daniel Logan before he gets her killed. You can save her if you convince her that leaving with you is the only way to keep Daniel and his kid alive.'"

At the bottom of the page was, "From a concerned friend."

Daniel tried not to react to the punch of raw emotion he got from hearing those words. But the emotion barreled through him, anyway. The SOB who'd written that letter had just threatened his daughter. It didn't matter if the threat weren't real because it still sank into him like a viper's fangs. He had to wrestle with the rage that came with that and then force himself to think like a cop.

"Sadie," Kara said on a rise of breath. Obviously, she was also having to deal with the firestorm cause by that letter.

"She's fine," Daniel reminded her. He reminded himself, too. His little girl was safe, and he had to deal with what this letter meant. Or figure out fast if it meant anything at all.

Kara reread the letter, muttering the words this time, while Daniel watched Sean for a reaction. If the man was acting, then he was doing a good job of it because his anger had morphed into what appeared to be worry. Some of Daniel's had morphed, too, and he'd mentally zoomed in on one line.

If you still care for Kara Holland, you'll get her away from Daniel Logan before he gets her killed.

That seemed to put this threat right in his lap. But was it?

Hell.

Maybe.

It was that possibility that had him rethinking this plan to be here at the inn. It had him rethinking everything.

"A concerned friend," Kara said, her voice mocking. "The killer. He didn't have my best interest at heart when he tried to murder us."

No. But this might not be from the killer. It could be some kind of sick game that Sean was playing. But why?

To get back at Kara and him?

Possibly. If so, that could point at Sean. At Eldon Stroud, too, if he wanted revenge for his daughter's death. Hell, Rizzo wasn't off that possible suspect list, either, since this could be just another way to torment them. Along with putting some suspicion on Sean.

Rizzo wasn't an idiot, and he would have known about the bad blood between Kara and Sean. Which meant there'd also be bad blood between Daniel and Sean. Rizzo could be trying to tap into that in some way by getting Sean involved in his already messy mix.

"Someone obviously wants you dead," Sean said, stating what was already way too obvious. He pointed to the letter. "It says if you leave Daniel that it'll keep you, him and his baby alive."

Daniel was certain that Kara hadn't missed that part. Certain, too, that she wasn't buying it. He got confirmation of that a moment later.

"This could be a ploy to separate Daniel and me so that it'll be easier to kill us," she said. She looked up from the letter and nailed her gaze to Sean. "Someone's murdering former surrogates, and why would my being with you stop something like that?"

"I could protect you," Sean blurted out.

Daniel's eyebrow rose, and he tapped his badge.

Sean huffed. "You don't have to be a cop to protect her. I could hire bodyguards." He turned to plead his case to Kara. "I wouldn't let a killer get to you. We were close once. Remember that, and maybe then you'll realize that I'd do anything to keep you safe."

"Daniel's doing everything possible to keep me safe," Kara argued.

Daniel hated that he felt any bit of pleasure about her saying that. But he did. Too bad he didn't have as much faith in himself as Kara did.

Sean huffed, propped his hands on his hips. "Does that mean you won't even consider going with me?"

"That's exactly what it means," Kara said without hesitation. "Do I have to remind you that you wanted nothing to do with me when I told you I was becoming a surrogate? Because I certainly don't have to be reminded of it. There's no way I can trust you after you did that."

Sean's next huff was a lot louder, and his eyes narrowed. "Fine, suit yourself, but remember this. If you stay, you're putting his daughter in danger. Is that what your sister would have wanted?" He slid them both a nasty glare. "Of course, I doubt Maryanne would have wanted you sleeping with Daniel, either."

Thankfully, Kara didn't bite on that last part

and try to convince Sean that they weren't lovers. Neither did Daniel, and their combined silence and hard stares must have made the man realize this was one argument he wouldn't win. Cursing them both, Sean turned and stormed out. Unfortunately, Sean nearly smacked right into Cybil, who was making her way up the steps.

"Kara's going to get them all killed," Sean grumbled, maybe to Cybil, maybe just to himself.

"A problem?" Cybil asked Daniel when she stepped in and closed the door behind her.

"Maybe." Daniel tipped his head to the letter that Kara was still holding. "Could you put that in an evidence bag and send it to the lab? Sean said someone sent it to him, and it might be connected to the murders."

"Of course," Cybil answered, heading right back out. "I've got a field bag in my SUV. I can bag it, and Leo can carry it back to the office for a courier to pick up."

Daniel thanked her, and Cybil headed out.

"Do you think Sean's right?" Kara muttered the moment his fellow deputy was out of earshot. "Do you really think I could get us all killed?"

"No." Daniel didn't even have to think before he answered. "Remember, both of us were attacked last night. I believe you were right when you said it'd be easier for someone to come after us if we weren't together. Especially if you were with bodyguards that Sean hired."

Meeting his gaze, Kara made a sound of agreement. "I don't trust Sean."

"Neither do I," Daniel immediately assured her.

He was glad they were on the same wavelength, but that didn't address the problem of keeping Kara safe while in his protective custody. And making sure that Sadie didn't get caught up in the crosshairs of a killer gunning for them. Moving his baby away from the ranch was a start, but he had to do more.

Daniel's phone rang just as Cybil was coming back into the house, and he answered it while he shut the door and reset the security alarm. It was Barrett, and Daniel put the call on speaker.

"I just got a call that Sean Maynard was at the inn," Barrett greeted.

That shouldn't have surprised Daniel. Mercy Ridge was filled with gossips, but in this case, the talk had happened darn fast since Sean had only been gone a couple of minutes.

"Sean brought Kara a letter that he claims he received this morning," Daniel explained. He watched as Cybil put on a pair of thin latex gloves to take both the letter and the envelope from Kara and slip them in an evidence bag. "Cybil's taking it now. I'll call the lab and see if they can put a rush on it."

"I can do that," Barrett offered.

Even better. As the sheriff, his brother had more pull than he did in that sort of thing.

"Rizzo's coming in," Barrett added a moment later. "This shouldn't come as a shock to you, but he's pissed. Really pissed. It makes me wonder if he's taking some kind of drug that's hyping him up."

"Maybe. Then again, Rizzo's usually riled about something." And being ordered in for a formal interview wouldn't sit well with him.

"True, but I might try to find a way to have him tested."

Daniel definitely didn't like the sound of that. "You're not going to bait Rizzo and have him throw a punch at you so you can arrest him, are you?"

"No, but that'd be easy enough to do. The man's on a short fuse. But he's bringing his lawyers. Yes, that's plural. *Lawyers*. So, I might be able to appeal to them to help clear their client's name with tests for gunshot residue and drugs. Maybe even a lie detector."

"Good luck with that," Daniel mumbled. He wasn't convinced, but if anyone could do that, it was Barrett. Maybe Barrett could press a few of Rizzo's hot buttons and get him to agree to the tests. Then again, if Rizzo was truly guilty, then there was no way that was happening.

Cybil finished bagging the letter, and she stepped into the living room with it to label the bag and start the record of the chain of custody. By labeling it and then logging it into the database, that would assure the courts and the legal system that the evidence had been handled properly.

"I just got a report back on Eldon Stroud," Barrett went on. "He's got a record. He threatened some of the staff at the hospital where his daughter died and then tried to assault one of the doctors."

Daniel thought about that for a moment. Such behavior could be an "excuse" for someone experiencing grief. "I'm surprised he didn't go after someone at the fertility clinic. I mean, other than sending a threatening letter."

"Oh, he did. Eldon threatened the former clinic director, Dr. Millie Hilburn. She retired about eight months ago, but she reported the threat to SAPD. The gist is that Eldon said he believed she should be punished for luring young women into surrogacy."

Punished could equal murder, and Daniel saw Kara shudder. He was right there with her. "Please tell me that SAPD has offered Dr. Hilburn protection?"

"They have, and she's taking it. She said she believes she saw Eldon following her a couple of times. SAPD hauled him in for questioning, but he insisted he had a right to watch the doctor. That's when she filed a restraining order. That's not his first one. The doctor he assaulted filed one, too."

"Has he served any time in jail?" Daniel asked.

"Two months, that's all, but he's on probation. That's why he doesn't have a choice about coming in for an interview."

Good. Maybe Barrett could use the man's parole to get some answers. Even if Eldon wasn't the person committing the murders, he might know something.

"I'll do a video feed of the interviews to your laptop," Barrett added a moment later. "Text me any questions you want me to ask them."

Daniel assured him that he would, and he

ended the call just as Cybil was heading upstairs. She had the evidence bag that she would give to Leo, and then Leo could finally get back to work. Daniel would do the same. He obviously had some calls, and decisions, to make. First, though, he needed to start with Kara while they had a moment alone.

"I'm sorry you're caught up in this," he said, placing his hand on her arm.

He would have said more, but she stopped him by shaking her head. "No, you're not going to apologize to me. I wanted to be a surrogate. I wanted to carry a child for Maryanne and you."

"But remember, this situation might be because of me," Daniel pointed out. "Because of Rizzo."

"Even if it is, you're not apologizing because someone has gone off half-cocked and might want you dead." She touched his hand that was still on her arm. "We'll work together and stop this person. We'll get justice for all the women he's killed."

She sounded resolved enough, but Daniel suspected she didn't want him to see just how shaken up she truly was.

The sound of the hurried footsteps on the stairs had both Kara and him whirling in that direction. It was Leo, and he wasn't carrying the bagged envelope but rather his gun.

"Sadie's all right," Leo immediately said as he raced down the stairs. "She's in the bathtub, and Noreen, Ellen and Cybil are all with her."

His brother's reassurance didn't help. Daniel's heart went into a gallop. "What's wrong? What happened?"

Leo ran past him, heading to take up position by the window. "Someone just spotted a gunman on the roof of the diner across the street."

Chapter Nine

Kara had been on an emotional roller coaster since learning the latest details about the missing and dead surrogates. But this was a threat that cut to the bone.

Because Sadie could be hurt.

Kara wanted to run upstairs to her, but Daniel motioned for her to get down on the floor. She did, but Daniel and Leo didn't. They each went to a window, and with their guns drawn and ready, they peered outside. She braced herself for the sounds of shots. For an attack. And she prayed that Leo or Daniel could take the guy out before he did any harm.

"Who reported the gunman?" Daniel asked.

"Gayla Howard," Leo answered from the other side of the room.

Kara knew her. She was a nurse who worked at the small hospital just up the street. She also lived in an apartment over the hardware store so it was possible Gayla had seen the man from there, and she'd called Leo because they were friends. Thank God she'd spotted him before shots had been fired. Main Street wasn't exactly a bustling place, but at this time of the day, there'd be people going to and from work and the shops.

"Gayla's safe?" Daniel pressed.

"Yeah," Leo answered. "I told her to stay put, and then I called Barrett. He's on the way to the back of the diner now. Jake's with him."

Jake Mendoza was the nighttime deputy, but obviously he'd stayed around after his shift. No doubt because Barrett had been busy with the murder investigation, and Leo and Daniel had been tied up keeping Sadie and Kara safe.

"Do you see the man?" Kara asked them.

"No," Leo and Daniel answered in unison, but the moment they spoke, the sound of Daniel's phone ringing shot through the room. Because every nerve in her body was on edge, Kara felt the surge of adrenaline and better positioned herself in case she needed to help protect Sadie.

"It's Barrett," Daniel said after giving her a glance. No doubt to make sure she was okay. She wasn't. But she didn't want him focused on her right now.

"The guy with the gun's gone," Barrett said the moment Daniel had him on speaker. "No sign of him."

"You're sure he was actually there?" Daniel pressed. He no doubt believed Gayla, but the nurse had to be on edge, too. Heck, everyone in town probably was. It was easy to blow things out of proportion and see threats that weren't there.

At least that's what Kara hoped had happened.

"Three people spotted a man wearing a dark hat and sunglasses on the roof," Barrett verified, dashing Kara's hopes. "Two of them saw the guy climbing down a rope ladder, but no one saw what direction he went. I'm putting out an alert for everyone to stay inside while Jake and I look for him."

"I'll help," Leo volunteered. "Cybil's upstairs with Sadie. Daniel's downstairs with Kara."

"Good," Barrett said. "Go out the back of the inn in case this guy still has the place in his sights. I've called in the reserve deputies, and there's a Texas Ranger on the way."

Kara was sure Barrett and his brothers would welcome the help, but those interviews with

Eldon and Rizzo were important, too. Because maybe one of them had hired this gunman.

Or maybe *one was* the gunman.

That seemed a huge risk for Rizzo to take since everyone in town knew him, but with the hat and sunglasses, he perhaps thought it was a chance worth taking. Especially if he'd managed to get off a shot that would have taken out Daniel or her. Of course, the hardest way to hit at Daniel and her would be to go after Sadie.

"I'll reset the security after you leave," Daniel said, following Leo into the back. "Stay down," he told Kara. "I won't be long."

She lifted her head to make eye contact with Daniel before he hurried after his brother. He'd been right about not being long. It took him less than a minute. But that was plenty of time for her worries to skyrocket about Sadie and him.

"What are we going to do about Sadie?" she asked when Daniel ran back through to get to the front window.

This time he didn't look at her, and even in profile she could see that this was tearing him to pieces. His jaw was set. His body tight and braced for a fight. He was going to have to make some hard decisions to keep Sadie safe.

So would she. Except it wouldn't be hard at all to put Sadie first.

"I could be bait," Kara insisted. "I could try to draw out the killer."

"That didn't go so well last time you tried it," he reminded her in a snap.

"No, but it's obvious the killer's getting more…daring," she said because she couldn't think of another word that didn't involve profanity. "He might not be able to resist coming after me if I make it easy for him."

"No," Barrett said before she even finished. "I'm not going to let you get close enough to this snake for him to try to finish you off."

"Then what?" She didn't want to die, but she also didn't want anyone hurt if she could do something to stop it. "I can do this. I can shoot and I know self-defense—"

"No," he repeated, and this time there was eye contact. Daniel shot her a glare for a split second before he turned back to the window. "But we are going to make some changes."

Before he could say what those changes would be, his phone rang. "It's Dispatch," he relayed to her, and she watched as he listened to whatever the person on the other end of the line was telling him. "Eldon Stroud wants to talk to me?" Daniel asked after a couple of seconds. "Put his call through."

Kara shook her head, not understanding why Eldon had phoned Daniel when it was Barrett who'd called him in for an interview. Daniel was clearly puzzled, too, but he took the call on speaker.

"Deputy Daniel Logan," he said when Dispatch switched over the call.

"You already know who I am," Eldon said. Considering his police record and the tone of his threats, Kara had expected the man to shout or spew some venom. But his voice was soft and maybe a little hoarse, the way someone might sound if they'd been sick.

"I do. Why are you calling?"

"I'm here in Mercy Ridge, and I thought you'd have things to say to me. When I found out you wouldn't be in the interview, I decided to get in touch."

"You're here in Mercy Ridge?" Daniel repeated. He checked the time, and Kara knew why. The man wasn't due in to interview until the afternoon, which was still several hours away. "By any chance, were you on the roof of the diner a few minutes ago?"

"No," Eldon answered without pausing or snarling at the question. "But I heard somebody was up there. I'm at the gas station now, and there's talk about it. We're all supposed to stay inside. Was the guy on the roof gunning for you?" he added after a short pause.

"You tell me. What do you know about that?"

"Nothing. I know what you think of me." Eldon's voice was still as calm as a lake. "I've been arrested, and I've spent some time in jail. I lost my daughter, and I've had some trouble dealing with that."

Now there was emotion. Eldon's voice cracked on the word *daughter* and the grief practically poured through. Kara understood that kind of grief. So did Daniel. They'd both lost Maryanne. But sometimes grief could make you do things you wouldn't normally do.

"I'll do the interview with your brother," Eldon went on. "From everything I'm hearing about him, he's a good man. Is he planning to arrest me for these murders y'all are investigating?"

Kara saw the quick debate on Daniel's face before he countered Eldon's question with one of his own. "What have you heard about the murders?" That was as cop-like as it could get.

"I've been reading about them in the newspapers. The girls were surrogates just like my daughter, and I have to wonder if they were messed over like my girl was."

"Messed over?" Daniel repeated. "How?"

"She was talked into doing that by a so-called friend," he answered without hesitation. "She carried another woman's baby for money, and the people at that clinic talked her into doing it."

Despite his personal grudge against surrogacy and the clinic, Eldon still never raised his voice. But the emotion was coming off him in thick waves.

"You blame the clinic for your daughter's death," Daniel said, and this time it wasn't a question.

"Yes." Eldon said that as gospel. "If she hadn't been talked into carrying a child, then she wouldn't have gotten the blood clot. She'd still be alive." Now, he paused. "Her mother died years ago. My daughter was all I had."

"I'm sorry," Daniel said. No cop voice that time. There was plenty of sympathy in his tone.

"I heard you lost your wife, too," Eldon went on after he muttered a thank-you. "It twists you up. It breaks you."

"It can. But I have a daughter, and I want

to keep her safe. Do you know who's trying to hurt her?"

"Somebody wants to hurt her?" Eldon blurted out.

"It looks that way. If the man on the roof of the diner had fired shots at us, he could have hit my little girl."

Eldon stayed quiet for several long moments. "The little girl you had with a surrogate. Your wife's sister, Kara Holland." And just like that, his tone changed. His voice was still low, but it was now laced with a fire and brimstone kind of judgment.

"My wife and I wanted a child, and her sister carried it for us," Daniel calmly pointed out. "Now, I have a child I love."

"You have her because of surrogacy." Again, that seemed to be some kind of judgment. "But the child shouldn't have to suffer because of the decisions the parents made."

Daniel waited, no doubt hoping Eldon would add more to that. When the man didn't, Daniel prompted him with a very direct question, "Do you know who's trying to hurt Kara, my daughter and me?"

"No," Eldon answered, and Kara so wished she was face-to-face with him so she could perhaps tell if he was lying. Or better yet, she wished Daniel could see him. He'd be a better judge if Eldon knew more than he was saying.

A muscle flickered in Daniel's already tight jaw. "How long have you been at the gas station?" he demanded.

Eldon made an audible sigh. "You're wanting to know if I have an alibi for the time that man was on the roof. Well, I don't. By the time I got to the gas station, the place was already buzzing of talk about it."

"And where were you this morning?" Daniel pressed, clearly checking to see if Eldon had an alibi for the time the dead woman had been left on the road.

"On the way here. No one I know saw me, and there's no one who'll vouch for what I'm saying. That's a problem for both of us. I can't prove my innocence, and you can't gather enough evidence to charge me with a crime."

"Not yet." That was clearly a warning, and Kara hoped it would shake Eldon enough that the man would spill something important during his interview with Barrett.

"I didn't make the bed you're lying in right now, Deputy Logan. You did. Sometimes, people have to deal with the consequences of their actions."

That sent a chill through her because it sounded very much like a threat.

"If you murdered those surrogates and came after Kara and me, then you'll have to deal with the consequences of your actions, too," Daniel warned him right back. "Not just prison time but a needle in the arm because you'll get the death penalty. Do you think that's the way to honor your daughter's memory?"

Kara held her breath, waiting to see if any of that had gotten through to Eldon, but she couldn't tell because he ended the call. While it was still fresh in her mind, she went back through the conversation, trying to pick out any details that would give away his guilt. Or his innocence. Nothing. She had no idea if Eldon was the killer who'd made Daniel and her his next target.

Before Daniel could even put his phone away, it rang again, and for a moment she thought it was Eldon calling them back. But it was Barrett's voice she heard when Daniel answered the call on speaker.

"There's no sign of the gunman," Barrett immediately said. "Every business owner on Main Street has checked in with Dispatch, and no one has seen him."

What Kara felt went well beyond disappointment. This sickened her and made her terrified for Daniel and Sadie.

"Jake's just searched the grounds around the inn," Barrett went on, "and it's clear. I suspect the guy left the area as soon as he came down off the roof of the diner."

Daniel made a sound of agreement, and she could see his shoulders drop. Again, not just disappointment but a weariness that the danger was far from being over.

"I'll keep Sadie upstairs a while longer," Daniel said. "By the way, Eldon just called me. He claims he's not behind the murders."

"Guilty men usually say that," Barrett grumbled with all the cynicism of a veteran cop.

"Yeah. He might have thought he was clearing his name by calling me, but I just moved him to the top of my suspect list. I'm thinking he called to taunt me because he missed out on firing shots into the inn."

"Where is he?" Barrett immediately asked.

"The gas station. Maybe you can get someone up there to see if he has a weapon in his vehicle. Maybe a dark cap and sunglasses, too, that match the description of what the gunman was wearing."

"I will. I'll get right back to you on that," Barrett assured him.

After another of those heavy sighs, Daniel moved away from the window and came back into the foyer with her. "Don't get your hopes up," he said. "If Eldon had those things, he probably ditched them before he ever went in the gas station. He'd know that he would be a suspect just by being in the area."

Kara had already thought of that, but until she heard Daniel say it aloud, she hadn't realized that she had indeed been hanging on to a glimmer of hope. It felt like another blow to have that taken away.

She tried not to show the disappointment and the barrage of other feelings that were coursing through her. It wouldn't help anyone if she didn't stay strong, but she knew she wasn't fooling Daniel. He was well aware of what she was going through, and that was probably why he pulled her into his arms.

Or so she thought that was why.

But then his mouth came to hers. Not for some chaste peck to comfort her. No. This was the real deal. A hot, hungry kiss. He parted her lips, tasting her. And she tasted him.

Oh, mercy. Daniel tasted as good as he looked.

Her body didn't forget the danger or the murders. Didn't forget that they had so much at stake. However, what he was doing to her kicked up the heat, turning it to a full blaze, and Kara let that fire slide through her. She wasn't sure how Daniel could manage to get her to flash point with just a kiss, but he did it. For a few moments, he made her body burn and her mind cloud.

He also made her want him more than her next breath.

And then he stopped.

He pulled back, looked down at her, and she could see the battle he was having with his own body. Could see something else, too.

The disgust.

Not for her but for himself. He hadn't wanted to kiss her, and he sure as heck hadn't wanted to feel this way. *Welcome to the club.* That kiss had just opened a box that probably should have stayed shut.

Daniel continued to stare down at her, and she saw the regret building. And she also saw something else that she couldn't quite decipher. Not until he spoke.

"I'm going to have to move Sadie to a safe house." Daniel said it fast as if ripping off a bandage from a still healing wound. "And you and I can't go with her."

Everything inside her went still, and she

took a moment to let that sink in. No, they couldn't go with her. Because they would just carry the threat with them. Carry the threat to Sadie.

Kara cleared her throat to make sure her voice would sound steady. "When will you take her?"

"It needs to be now," Daniel said, and he started for the stairs.

Chapter Ten

Daniel figured that kissing Kara was about the stupidest thing he could have done. He should have been keeping an emotional barrier between them and not skyrocketing the attraction. But he would have to kick himself for it later.

For now, he had only one priority and that was to keep his daughter safe.

While he made his way up the stairs to check on Sadie and the others, he called Leo, and was grateful that his brother answered on the first ring. "I want to move Sadie to a safe house right away."

Leo didn't question that, and the demand probably wasn't a surprise. The night before, Leo and he had had a phone conversation about this very possibility. Daniel had wanted to try the inn first, but that was for purely selfish reasons. He wanted to be with his little girl and have her close to his family. However, he couldn't take that kind of risk, not with a gunman obviously knowing their location.

"I'll get everything ready," Leo assured him. "I can be ready to leave in fifteen minutes."

He felt some of the tightness ease up in his chest. "Thanks."

Daniel took a moment to gather his breath and stopped in the hall to finish the conversation with Leo before going in to see Sadie. "Since Barrett and the other deputies are tied up right now, Kara and I will follow Noreen, Cybil, Sadie and you to the safe house. Maybe even Ellen, too, if I can talk her into going. That way, I can make sure the killer isn't following you. Once we're sure everything is okay at the safe house, then Kara and I will come back here."

Leo cursed. "You're not trying to draw out the killer and make him come after you?"

Kara had offered herself up to do just that, but if anyone was drawing out a killer, he would be the one to do it. Still, Daniel kept that to himself. "I just need to put some distance between Sadie and me."

"I get that, but it means Kara and you will be doing the return trip without backup."

Daniel hated to use Kara's argument, but he

would. He didn't want to pull Cybil or Leo off protection detail for Sadie. "Kara's an expert marksman." At least she was if the gossips had gotten it right. "We'll come straight back here from the safe house."

Which would only take about thirty minutes.

However, it'd take them much longer to get to the safe house since they would essentially have to drive around to make sure no one was on their tails. That would mean Daniel missing the video interviews with their three suspects, but it couldn't be helped.

"I'll be at the inn as soon as I can," Leo finally said. His brother's quick goodbye likely didn't mean Leo was giving up his argument about Kara and him not having backup, but at least he wasn't wasting any more time.

Daniel found Cybil and Noreen sitting on the bathroom floor, and they'd put Sadie in the bathtub along with a stash of toys. She was playing and was thankfully unaware of the scare they'd just had.

"Ellen's in the room across the hall getting some books for Sadie," Cybil explained. "I got a text from Barrett saying the gunman wasn't around so I thought it was okay for her to leave the bathroom."

Daniel silently cursed himself for the reminder that Ellen was also in danger. “It’s okay,” he assured her as both Ellen and Kara stepped into the doorway. He was glad he had them all there because he wouldn’t have to repeat himself.

“We’ll be leaving for a safe house in a few minutes,” Daniel explained. He looked at Sadie when she grinned at him, and it nearly broke his heart. Since she’d been born, he hadn’t gone a full day without seeing her, but that could change.

And all because of a killer.

“I’d like for you to go with them to the safe house,” he added to Ellen.

The woman didn’t hesitate. Maybe because she’d just gotten the scare of her life with that gunman. “I’ll pack a bag,” Ellen said, hurrying off after she handed the children’s book she’d been holding to Kara.

Kara took the book to Sadie, sat down on the edge of the tub and began thumbing through the pages with her.

“Kara and I will follow the cruiser, but we’ll be coming back here to the inn. There’ll be some toiletries and some clothes at the safe house,” he went on, talking to Cybil now, “but if you need anything from your place, make a list."

"I have a bag in my SUV," she said. "I wasn't sure how long I'd be staying here at the inn so I packed one."

"Good thinking." He was about to go with her to get it, but he thought of something. "Maybe I can drive your SUV to the safe house and then bring it back here?"

"Of course," she said, fishing out the keys from her pocket and handing them to him. She eyed him, though, with the same concern that Daniel suspected he'd get from Leo. "Kara and you will be careful," she added as a reminder.

Yeah, they would be, but it didn't mean he could keep Kara out of harm's way. She wouldn't want that, though, if it came at Sadie's expense.

Now that everyone knew what was going on, Daniel took Noreen's suitcase that hadn't yet been unpacked, and he headed downstairs to wait for Leo. He didn't have to wait long. Leo was pulling up in the cruiser at the back of the inn as Daniel made it into the kitchen. He disarmed the security just long enough to get Leo inside and made a sweeping glance around the yard.

"You didn't make a mistake bringing Sadie

here," Leo said right off. His brother had obviously picked up a lot from his tone over the phone. "We had to know how fast the killer would respond. Now, we know."

Yeah, now they knew. Or maybe they did. If the person on the roof had been the actual killer, then why hadn't he taken a shot? Even getting off one shot could have done some damage. Or worse. It could have killed someone inside.

Daniel doubted the shooter had simply changed his mind. No. It was more likely that he'd realized he had been spotted and hadn't wanted to take the risk of being gunned down himself. After all, many people in Mercy Ridge carried some kind of weapon.

At the sound of footsteps behind them, Leo and Daniel turned in that direction to see Kara coming in. She exchanged a quick glance with Daniel, but apparently it wasn't quick enough for Leo not to notice that something was, well, different between them. Leo lifted his eyebrow in a way that made Daniel realize that his brother was also picking up on his expressions.

"Don't ask," Daniel warned him when Leo opened his mouth.

Leo just shrugged and winked at Kara. His brother's attempt to lighten things up, though, didn't last. He got very serious when Noreen came into the room with Sadie. Cybil and Ellen were right behind them.

"I can turn on the security system with my phone once we're in the cruiser," Ellen offered.

Daniel nodded and was thankful for the feature. That way, someone wouldn't be able to just sneak in and lie in wait while Kara and he were gone.

"Get in the cruiser as fast as you can," Daniel instructed them. "Kara and I will go out front and get in Cybil's SUV." He gave Sadie a kiss on the cheek, but he tried not to linger too long. He'd be able to say goodbye to her once they were at the safe house.

Leo didn't waste any time, either. He got Noreen, Ellen, Sadie and Cybil out the back door. Daniel waited until they were all inside the cruiser before he locked the back door and hurried to the front with Kara. He drew his gun and wasn't surprised when Kara did the same. He set the lock on the door, and they ran.

Daniel held his breath every step of the way from the inn's front door to the cruiser, and he prayed Barrett was right about there not being any signs of the gunman having stuck around. Cybil's SUV was in the front spot in the parking lot. Not far in distance but plenty far enough.

Kara and he jumped into the SUV and had a couple of seconds to steady themselves before Leo drove out ahead of them. Daniel followed, knowing that he'd stay on edge every second of this trip. As they drove by the shops, both Kara and he glanced at each one. If there were going to be attack, Daniel hoped the person would come after Kara and him and leave the cruiser alone.

"You told Leo that you kissed me?" Kara asked.

Daniel did a mental double take at her question, and it took him a moment to realize that she was trying to ease the thick tension in the air. Of course, talk of kissing her wasn't exactly a tension-breaking subject.

"No, but I believe Leo guessed that's what happened," Daniel answered. Heck, maybe Leo thought it was more than just a kiss and that Kara and he were now lovers. Or soon would be.

He wasn't sure what to think of the small sound she made, and he couldn't see her face to try to gauge her expression. Kara continued to look around, studying their surroundings.

It didn't take long for them to get out of town

and onto the road that led to Daniel's ranch, but he knew they wouldn't be going there. Leo would drive past it and keep going for at least ten miles before he started a series of turns that would let them see if anyone was following them. It would be much easier to do that on a country road where the houses were few and far between.

"The safe house can't be linked to any of us," Daniel explained, hoping to relieve her mind a little. Hoping, too, that the reminder would also give him some relief. "It's a place the Marshals set up when they had someone going into witness protection. The witness moved out months ago, but the Marshals kept it in case they or we had to use it."

"So, the safe house is close?" she asked.

"It's in the county about twenty miles from here." So, not nearly close enough, considering that's where Sadie would be.

When they drove by the road to his ranch, Daniel took another look around. He didn't see anyone, but then his house wasn't visible from here. However, he did see one of his ranch hands out in the pasture. He was on horseback and had a rifle sheathed in a saddle case. Obviously, the hand was on alert just as Kara and he were.

They'd only gone about another mile when Daniel saw Leo tap his breaks. His attention immediately slashed to the road ahead. Nothing. But then he caught the blur of motion out of the corner of his eye.

A woman.

She was wearing jeans and a white top, and she was running through a pasture. She was throwing glances over her shoulder as if someone were in pursuit.

"Who is that?" Kara asked, automatically moving closer to the window.

"I don't know," he said.

Just as the sound rang out. Daniel didn't have to guess what the sound was.

A gunshot.

KARA THOUGHT MAYBE her heart had stopped for a few seconds. It seemed as if everything stopped except for that horrible sound that had blasted through the air. Her breath stalled in the throat. Her muscles froze. Still, her first thought was that Sadie could be hurt.

She forced herself to remain calm and checked their surroundings. The shot hadn't gone into the cruiser. Not into the SUV, either. But it had hit something else. Kara watched as the bright red blood spread across the running woman's back. She stumbled, nearly fell, but she regained her balance and kept on running. Kara could see the sheer terror on the woman's face.

And the woman saw them, too.

Despite her obvious injury, she started running toward the cruiser and the SUV.

Another shot came, and Kara fought her way through the shock to try to pinpoint the location of the shooter. She thought maybe he was in the thick woods on the other side of the road. But she couldn't see him. And he'd almost certainly be out of range of their handguns. She was pretty sure whoever was firing those shots was using a rifle.

With his gun ready, Daniel took out his phone and pressed in Leo's number. "Keep going," he told Leo the moment he was on the line. He slowed to a stop on the narrow gravel shoulder of the road and used the phone to motion for Kara to move lower onto the seat. "Get Sadie out of here now."

"What are you going to do?" Leo demanded.

"I'm going to try to save that woman," Daniel answered without pausing a beat. "Call Barrett and get me some backup out here. Call my ranch hands, too, since they can get here faster. But hit the accelerator and keep going."

Kara doubted that Leo wanted to leave his brother and her behind, but he was in charge of precious cargo so he did just as Daniel asked. Kara did drop lower in the seat, but only a couple of inches so she could still keep watch. From over the dashboard, she saw the cruiser speed away.

"You stay down," Daniel warned her, and he hit the latch to put her seat in a near reclining position.

"I can't give you backup like this," she reminded him.

"You're not leaving this SUV," he insisted.

With Daniel's gaze firing into the woods where the shooter no doubt was, he practically climbed over Kara to get to the door on her side. Once he had it open, he got out, his boots thudding when they hit the gravel. The SUV itself would give him some cover, but he could still be shot. Especially if he did what Kara believed he would do.

He was going out into that pasture to rescue the woman.

"Help me," the woman called out.

Kara risked looking at her, and the thin brunette was still coming toward them. Not fast, though, and she was stumbling now and weaving around. Maybe because of the blood loss or the shock of the gunshot wound. She still couldn't clearly see the woman's face, but Kara had to consider the worst-case scenario.

That this attack was connected to the surrogates.

Another shot blasted through the air, causing the woman to scream. The sound turned Kara's blood to ice, and she wasn't sure she could just sit there and let the woman be killed.

"Stay put," Daniel warned her one last time.

Even though there was another blast, he crouched down some and started making his way to the woman. Kara eased up in the seat just enough to watch them. She also lifted her gun, and her gaze snapped toward the woods when there was another shot. So far, none of the bullets had gone into the SUV, but that could change once he hit his target.

The woman.

This brunette was clearly the one he wanted because Kara could see the bullets kicking up the dirt around her. Unfortunately, Daniel was headed right into the path of those shots. At the moment, he might not be the shooter's primary target, but that could change.

The next shot landed even closer than the others. So close that Daniel had to shield his eyes because of the debris from it that flew into his face. He still hadn't reached the woman, and worse, she'd stopped. She was obviously struggling just to stay on her feet.

God, she could be dying. Bleeding to death.

And the shots just kept coming.

Kara had had enough. This time it wasn't fear that sliced through her but rage. No way would Daniel approve of what she was doing, but she needed to create a diversion if he had any chance of rescuing the woman.

She leaned over, rolled down the window of the SUV took aim at the area where she thought the shooter was. Even though she seriously doubted she could actually hit the gunman from this distance, she fired, anyway.

Then she fired again. And again.

The sound from her own shots was deafening in the small space of the SUV, and it caused a sharp pain to pierce through her ears. It was hard to hear, but she didn't miss that the gunman hadn't fired any shots. That's why she sent another two bullets in his direction.

Kara prayed that it had caused him to go on the run even though she would have preferred to stop this monster. She wanted to confront him. But that would have to wait. For now, Daniel and this injured woman had to come first.

"Get down!" Daniel shouted, and Kara was certain he meant that for her.

She did get down but not before she shifted her attention to check on Daniel. The woman was still on her feet. Not for long, though. Kara watched as she crumpled and fell to the ground.

"Call an ambulance," Daniel yelled.

Kara had to fumble through her purse, but she came up with her phone and called nine-one-one. "We need an ambulance," she said, rattling off their location.

Her throat froze, though, when she saw the vehicle in the rearview mirror. For a few terrifying moments, she thought the gunman was returning to try to finish them off.

But it was Tanner Parnell, Daniel's ranch hand.

He was definitely a welcome sight, and she was thankful they'd been so close to Daniel's ranch so that Tanner could get here this fast. And he was obviously ready to help. He bareled out of his truck, a rifle in hand.

"The shooter was over there," Kara said, pointing to the woods. "But I think he's gone now. Please be gone," she added in a whisper. She didn't want them all gunned down.

Tanner nodded, shifted his attention to Daniel, who was leaning over the injured woman. He headed toward them. So did Kara, and she saw Daniel strip off his shirt and use it to try to staunch the wound. By the time Kara made it to them, though, his shirt was already soaked with blood.

The woman was bleeding out.

Kara got a better look at her face now. She still didn't recognize her, but she appeared to be in her early twenties and had a slim build. There wasn't an ounce of color left in her. A stark contrast to the bright red of the blood on her clothes and Daniel's shirt.

Kara dropped down to her knees and helped Daniel apply some pressure to the wound. Tanner stood over them, keeping watch of the woods and the rest of the pasture.

"Who are you?" Daniel demanded. "Who did this to you?"

"Daisy," she answered, her voice barely audible. "Daisy Burkhart."

Daniel glanced up at Kara to see if she recognized the name, but she had to shake her head. "You were a surrogate?" Kara asked, and she braced herself for the gut punch she knew she was going to get.

Daisy gave a weak nod. "He killed me, didn't he?" she murmured. "I'm dying, aren't I?"

"He?" Daniel repeated. "Who did this to you, Daisy?"

The woman's eyelids fluttered down, and with the last breath she'd ever take, she whispered something.

The name of her killer.

Chapter Eleven

Sean Maynard.

Daniel wasn't sure who'd been more surprised—Kara or him—when Daisy had muttered that name. Of course, Sean had been a suspect since he'd shown up at the inn that morning, but Daniel had put Rizzo and Eldon way ahead of him. Judging from her shock, so had Kara.

He was sure the shock was still there as he sat in the bathroom of the inn and listened to the water in her shower. Daniel hadn't wanted to leave her alone once they'd made it back, but he'd understood when she'd said she had to wash off the blood.

Daisy Burkhart's blood.

Seeing it was a reminder that there was yet another dead surrogate. A murder that he hadn't been able to stop. And it sickened him to the core.

At least Sadie was safe, and that was a huge weight off him. Leo had done as Daniel asked, and he'd gotten Sadie and the others to the safe house. He'd done that, though, with backup from the Rangers since Daniel had stayed with Daisy's body until the CSIs and another team of Rangers had arrived.

While Daniel had still been at the scene, he'd also started the ball rolling on some new security measures. He'd had one of his hands make a quick trip to San Antonio to buy a dozen motion-activated cameras that were now placed on the tops of the buildings around the inn. If anyone tried to get on the roofs, the cameras would trigger an alert that would be sent to his phone.

Once Daniel had finally been able to get Kara back to Mercy Ridge, he'd brought her to the inn and locked down the place. That didn't mean a gunman couldn't still fire shots into the inn, but at least now Sadie wouldn't here.

And there was something else. Something that could work in their favor.

Maybe it'd been a fluke, but the person who'd killed Daisy hadn't been that good of a shot. He'd missed far more often than he'd hit, and he hadn't even tried to shoot Kara and him. This was despite Kara firing at him and

Daniel being out in the open where he'd been an easy target.

So, the question was—had Sean been the person pulling the trigger?

Was Kara's ex the killer responsible for all those deaths?

If so, that would make him a serial killer, but it left Daniel with a lot of questions. If Sean was behind this, then his motive had to be getting back at Kara for ditching him. Then why hadn't he simply tried to kill her in the pasture today? Why had he allowed Daisy to find out who he was?

Of course, it was possible all this was a ruse, that the real killer had told Daisy that he was Sean. It was also possible that the shooter was just a hired gun and not the same person responsible for murdering the other surrogates. But if the surrogate killer had been the one pulling the trigger today, then he didn't seem to have any decent sniper skills. That was a good thing for Kara and him. Still, they couldn't take any risks since the shooter didn't necessarily have to be good, just lucky.

Using his phone, he read through an email from Barrett and was trying to force his mind off the dead woman's face and her plea for help when Kara stepped from the shower. He automatically glanced up but just as quickly looked away. Kara wasn't naked but it was close. She had only a towel wrapped around her so he got a glimpse of plenty of bare arms and legs before she put on a robe.

"Your turn," she said. Her voice was strained. With reason. She'd just witnessed a woman being murdered, but Daniel thought some of her nerves were because they were sharing the very small bathroom.

She stepped around him, which was no easy feat, and of course, she ended up brushing against him. Daniel caught a whiff of the shampoo and soap, but her own scent was mixed in there, as well. He tried his best to ignore that. Tried his best to ignore the tug in his body that made him want to reach out and touch her.

"Has Barrett brought Sean in for questioning yet?" she asked.

"A Texas Ranger picked him up and is on the way to the sheriff's office now. Barrett will text me right before the interview starts."

Kara took up the position he'd just left. On the floor with her back against the door. She looked at everything but him, which was a good thing because he started to strip, starting with the loaner T-shirt that he'd gotten from one of the EMTs. His own shirt had been soaked with blood, and the Rangers had bagged it in case it'd picked up any fibers or trace from Daisy's body.

"I got some updates while you were in the shower," he started, shucking off the rest of his clothes. "Sadie's doing great. Leo said she's having a ball since she's got so many people willing to read to her and play with her."

"Good." She sounded relieved. But still tense. He figured that if there were any kind of unusual sound right now, she'd probably jump out of her skin. Or out of that bathrobe.

He didn't want to think about that.

However, imagining Kara's naked body was a whole lot better than some of the other images going through his head.

"The security cameras are all in place on the buildings," he went on.

"You'll be able to see if anyone goes up on one of the roofs?" she asked.

"Yeah. And two of the cameras are angled to pick up anyone coming to the front or back doors here at the inn. If anyone gets on a roof or comes to the doors, my phone will beep with an alert. That should give us time to take cover."

Well, take cover in her case. If he got an

alert and pinpointed the killer, then Daniel would try to put an end to this.

"Barrett's phone will beep, too, if any of the cameras are triggered. And he's shifted the times of the interviews," Daniel continued a moment later. "So we'll be able to watch them on my computer. He wants to talk to Sean first, before interviewing the others."

That made sense because if Sean confessed, then there'd be no need to interrogate Eldon and Rizzo. But Daniel didn't see Sean just owning up to murdering at least four women along with attempted murder and attacks on a cop and on his ex-girlfriend.

"If Sean's guilty, why wouldn't he have just run?" he heard Kara ask.

It was the million-dollar question. Daniel had an answer, but he wasn't sure it was the right one. "He would have looked guilty had he run. This way, he can claim his innocence and say that someone's trying to frame him."

And someone could be trying to do just that.

Daniel kept going through those *why* questions that were plaguing him. Why would Sean have let Daisy know who he was? Maybe it'd been for sport, to up the stakes of this cat-and-mouse game. Or maybe it'd just been a mistake. Daisy could have recognized him when he kidnapped her and then managed to get away from him. But that just led him to another why.

Why had Sean and Daisy been so close to his ranch?

He lathered up and quickly rinsed off. "Maybe Sean took Daisy to my place to kill her," he muttered, not figuring Kara would hear him.

But she did.

"It would be a way to hit at both you and me," Kara said. "Sean could have been planning on putting Daisy's body in your house or on your land."

Yeah, but if so, it was stupid when he had ranch hands working today. Then again, maybe Sean hadn't known that. Neither would Eldon. But Rizzo certainly would have.

He turned off the shower, wrapping a towel around his waist before he got out. No robe for him. There'd only been one in the bathroom, and Kara had used it. Maybe being nearly naked wouldn't give his body any bad ideas about Kara before he managed to get dressed.

"Barrett confirmed that Daisy Burkhart was a surrogate at Willingham Fertility Clinic," Daniel went on. No surprise there, but it was something that had to be checked off the list.

"She lived alone but was engaged. SAPD is questioning her fiancé, but they don't believe he was involved in this. He has a solid alibi since he was in a meeting with four other people at the time of Daisy's death."

Still keeping her eyes off him, Kara stood so they could go back into the bedroom. They were sharing it, as well. For now. That's because he didn't want her to be too far away from him if there was an attack. But in a couple hours when it was time for them to sleep, he'd have to figure out how to handle that. Daniel was 100 percent sure that he wouldn't be able to keep his hands, and his mouth, off her if they ended up in the same bed.

Kara took some fresh clothes from her suitcase and went into the walk-in closet to dress. Daniel stayed in the bedroom itself and did the same, using some clothes that Barrett had sent over for him. However, he hurried.

The moment he'd finished dressing, he put back on his holster and weapon and then went to the window to look out. This room had a good vantage point where he could see the entire backyard and parking lot. No one was lurking around, but Daniel figured if there was an attack, it'd come from the side or the front.

The shooter might get up on another nearby roof and start firing.

His truck was no longer in the parking lot. Thanks to Barrett, there was now a cruiser, a safer option if Kara and he had to make a run for it. Maybe, though, it wouldn't come down to that.

He turned when Kara finally came out of the closet. She was wearing jeans and a loose cotton top, and her hair was still wet from her shower.

And she was crying.

Judging from the way she quickly wiped the tears away, she probably hadn't wanted him to see that. He started toward her, but she waved him away.

"I'll stop," she insisted. "You don't need this."

"Neither do you. Sometimes, though, we can't control things." Which, of course, described him to a tee. He wasn't controlling much of anything right now. Including these thoughts he kept having about Kara.

It was stupid for him to pull her into his arms. Even more stupid to kiss her. But that's exactly what he did. He caught her sound of surprise with his mouth and deepened the kiss. Her stiff shocked response didn't last long.

Nope.

With his thoughts of her whirling and the air charged with sparks of lightning, Kara practically melted into him. Mouth to mouth. Body to body. And the sparks just kept on flying.

It'd been years since he'd kissed a woman like this. With a need that was already so hungry that it felt as if he could take her where she stood. Hc ached for Kara. Needed her. But worse, he wanted her now.

Daniel expected to feel a flood of guilt over kissing his late wife's sister. In fact, he thought he would have welcomed it because it would have forced him to take a huge step back and rethink this. But no guilt came. Only the heat that kept building and building.

Kara didn't help with getting him to step back. Just the opposite. Her arms went around him, and she pulled him closer, fitting him against her in a way that let him know she'd lost the willpower battle, too.

He could blame that lost battle on the spent adrenaline, the danger. The overwhelming fear that neither of them might live to see another day, but it kept going back to that want. His body had been simmering for her for days now. Maybe longer. And she was right here for the taking.

She slid her hand down his back, her fingers

digging into his skin, and she made a silky moan of pleasure. A sound that went straight to his groin. Hell, he was already harder than stone, and Kara had obviously noticed that, too, because she pressed her center against his.

Because his heartbeat was crashing in his ears, it took Daniel a moment to realize the next sound he heard was his phone ringing. He had to pull himself out of the lust trance he was in, and he cursed himself for the lapse. There were too many things going on for him to be kissing Kara.

"It's Barrett," he relayed to Kara, and he put the call on speaker. Also to put some distance between them, he went to the window again and glanced outside.

"Sean's in the interview room," Barrett said the moment he was on the line. "You can log into the feed to watch it. FYI, the Rangers have found nothing in Daisy's phone records to indicate she knew Sean. Her fiancé says he never heard her mention the man's name."

That didn't mean Sean hadn't been the one to kill her, but Daisy had certainly learned his name from somewhere. Or rather she'd learned the name the killer wanted her to.

Daniel went to the small desk where he'd put his laptop, and he booted it up. "Have the

CSIs gone into the woods where the shooter was?" he asked.

"They're there now, and we should have a preliminary report soon," Barrett answered. "Remember to text me any questions you want me to ask Sean. I'm going into the interview now."

Daniel hit the end-call button and logged into the video feed. Sean was seated at the metal table. Brandon Mauer, one of the town's two attorneys, was next to him, and he was making notes on a legal pad. Sean's attention, however, was nailed to the camera. He didn't appear angry—that was a surprise—but he was looking into the lens as if he wanted to send some kind of message.

Maybe to Kara.

Barrett came into the room, and he set up the interview by identifying everyone for the recording and reading Sean his rights. Sean spoke the moment Barrett had finished.

"I didn't kill anyone," Sean insisted. "And I have an alibi."

His lawyer laid his hand on Sean's arm, probably to tell his client to wait for the questions before he said anything, but Sean only continued.

"I was on the phone with a rancher who's

selling me some cattle when the attack was taking place," Sean added.

"What time was that?" Barrett countered. "And how do you know what time the attack happened?"

"It happened four hours ago," Sean provided without hesitating. "Something like that gets around so that's how I know. I was on the phone with Mason Ryland over in Silver Creek."

Barrett slid a notepad toward Sean. "Write down his name and contact info. I'll check with him." He gave Sean a moment to do that. "But a phone call doesn't prove your innocence. You could have had that conversation on your cell and still been in the area of the attack. Or you could have finished your business with Ryland and then gone to those woods where you gunned down a woman."

"No." Sean didn't shout his denial. He repeated it and buried his face in his hands for a couple of seconds. "I didn't gun anyone down."

Barrett gave him a flat cop's stare. "The dead woman said differently. In fact, her dying words were your name."

"My client didn't know the deceased." Brandon spoke up. "And there's no physical evidence to link him to this crime."

"Not yet. The scene's still being processed so something might turn up." Barrett combed his gaze over Sean. "The Ranger who brought you in said you'd just gotten out of the shower when he arrived at your place."

Sean shrugged. "So?"

"So, you might have done that to remove any gunshot residue," Barrett reminded him.

"No." This time Sean's voice was a little louder, and the huff he made sounded to be of pure frustration. "I told the Ranger that after my conversation with Ryland, I went for a ride on a new horse. I got sweaty and showered."

"I can't tell if he's lying," Kara muttered. "I should be able to tell."

There was plenty of frustration in her voice, too, and Daniel wanted to assure her that she shouldn't have been able to tell something like that. Some people were just good liars, and Sean might be one of them.

"My client has agreed to submit to a GSR test," Brandon stated. "He also agreed to come here and answer your questions, but as you well know, it's not necessary for him to prove his innocence."

"Yeah, yeah," Barrett grumbled. "I know the burden of proving his guilt is on me, but I've got a good start. I've got a murdered woman who told a cop that your client had killed her."

"A woman who could have been mistaken," Brandon was quick to point out. "After all, she was dying. She could have been confused. Or maybe her real killer wanted her to believe he was my client."

Sean's gaze fired back to the camera. "Is Kara listening to this?" he asked, ignoring everything his lawyer had just said.

"Yes, Kara Holland is watching," Barrett confirmed, giving her full name for the record. "So is my brother Deputy Daniel Logan."

Sean stood, his eyes staring right into the camera lens. "Kara, I didn't kill that woman. I swear, I didn't. I love you, and I want to make sure you're safe. Please let me see you. I need to talk to you."

Daniel looked at her, and after one glance he could tell that Kara was considering it. "He could be a killer," Daniel pointed out. "He could want to see you to finish whatever sick plan he's set in motion."

She nodded. "I don't intend to see him, but I would like to talk to him." Kara shifted her attention to Daniel. "I might be able to make him angry enough that he'll spill something."

"Does that mean you think he could have committed these murders and attacked us?"

Kara shook her head, sighed. "I just don't know. That's another reason for me to talk to him. I might be able to tell if we're talking."

Daniel cursed the pang of jealousy he got—but hell, it was there. Yeah, Kara and Sean had been lovers, and he shouldn't resent that. She was a grown woman and had a right to a life. But because of those kisses, Kara felt like, well, *his*. Which made him an idiot. A couple of kisses didn't equal a commitment or a relationship. Neither did the feelings he now had for her. But Daniel could see that's where they were heading.

And he had to stop it.

At least temporarily nix it, anyway. Once the murders were solved and he had Sadie safely back home, then he could figure out if things were going anywhere with Kara. He very much wanted things to go somewhere with her. Of course, his body was pushing for sex, and Daniel figured his body was going to get its way on that. It'd be different if Kara had been sending him "hands off" signals, but she wasn't. Just the opposite. There was plenty of need in her eyes.

Daniel texted Barrett, explaining that Kara

wanted to speak with Sean. He saw the same hesitation on his brother's face that he was sure had been on his own. A few snail-crawling moments went by before Barrett nodded and fired off a reply.

"Tap into the audio function on the camera feed," Barrett instructed.

Daniel did, and when he was done, Barrett turned back to Sean. He pointed to the small speaker below the camera. "Kara wants to talk to you."

Sean actually sat up straighter in his chair. He had what Daniel could only call a hopeful expression. "Kara? Did you hear what I said?"

"I did," she assured him. "Did you kill that woman? Did you kill any of the surrogates?"

Daniel could see the hope drain away from Sean's face. "No. You shouldn't have to ask me that. We were together for a long time. Years," he emphasized. "You know the kind of man I am."

Yeah, Kara knew he could be stubborn and mean. Maybe even obsessed. But that didn't make him a killer.

"Do you know anything about the surrogate murders or the attack on Daniel and me?" she pressed, obviously skipping over what he'd just told her.

"No." Now the anger flared through his eyes. "I love you. I wouldn't hurt you."

Daniel couldn't help but notice that Sean hadn't included him in that *I wouldn't hurt you*.

"I want us to get back together," Sean went on, standing now. "I can protect you." He muttered some profanity. "I believe someone is committing these murders to get back at Daniel. That's why you should get as far away from him as you can. You sure as hell shouldn't be staying with him."

"I'm not getting back together with you," she said without a shred of doubt in her voice. There wasn't any in her eyes, either, but Sean couldn't see that. The video feed was only one-way. "And why exactly do you think the murders are to get back at Daniel?"

"He's a cop," Sean answered so fast that he must have given it some thought. "I think someone he pissed off or arrested is doing this, and you're caught up in the middle of it. I'm caught up, too, because someone obviously tried to frame me."

Since Sean seemed to be getting more agitated with each word, Brandon took hold of his arm to pull him back in his seat. Sean just threw off his grip and kept his attention glued to the camera.

"I'm not leaving Daniel," Kara said. Then she paused and gave Daniel a look that he couldn't quite make out. She had something up her sleeve, and before he could ask what, she continued, "I have feelings for him."

As a declaration of love, it was pretty tame, but Sean clearly got the gist of it. Or rather the gist of what she wanted him to believe, that is. She'd basically just laid down the law and told her ex that she had a new man in her life.

A man Sean hated to the bone.

"Feelings for him," Sean spat out like the words were distasteful. His stare turned to a glare, and once again he shook off Brandon's attempt to have him sit. "Feelings for a man who could get you killed. I thought you were smarter than that, Kara."

"Oh, I'm smart," she countered. "That's why we're no longer together. That's why we'll never be together again," she amended. "Killing women and attacking me won't cause me to come running back to you."

Sean made a feral sound that came deep from within his throat. "If I were you, I'd be very careful." And it sounded very much like a threat.

Obviously, Brandon heard the threat, too, because he stood and angled himself so that he got in Sean's face. Daniel couldn't hear what Brandon whispered to his client, but it caused Sean to give an angry shake of his head.

"My client and I need a couple of minutes," Brandon said, and this time he took a firmer grip on Sean's arm. "Is it okay if we use the break room?"

"Sure," Barrett answered, his voice far from friendly. "Just don't leave the building." His brother waited until Sean and Brandon were out of the room before he looked up at the camera. "I'm going to my office to call this Mason Ryland and see if he can confirm Sean's alibi. I'll text you when the interview starts back up."

"Thanks," Daniel muttered, and he was about to pause the video feed when he heard a sound. A series of three sharp beeps.

And he drew his gun.

Because someone had just triggered a security camera.

Chapter Twelve

Kara drew her gun, and beside her, Daniel did the same. He also whipped out his phone and pulled up the small split screens for the security cams. It didn't take them long to see who'd triggered the alarm.

Rizzo.

Daniel and she cursed at the same moment, and she wasn't surprised when Rizzo knocked on the door again. It was louder this time and followed by the man's equally loud voice.

"I need to talk to you, Daniel. I think you'll want to hear what I have to say."

That brought on more cursing from Daniel, and he headed down the stairs. "Stay back," he warned her.

At least he hadn't told her to stay put upstairs. Something Kara wouldn't have done. If Rizzo was there to attack them, Daniel would need backup.

"Lift your hands so I can see them," Daniel ordered their visitor, and he didn't go to the door to verify that Rizzo had done it and that he wasn't armed. Instead, Daniel watched the man on the camera feed on his phone.

No gun in sight. Of course, that didn't mean Rizzo wasn't carrying. Still, it'd be stupid to come to the inn door in plain sight of the cameras and the people on Main Street.

Daniel's phone rang, and he hit the answer button while he eyed Rizzo from the window.

"Is everything okay?" she heard Barrett ask. "The alarm went off for one of the cameras."

"Rizzo's here. I'll see what he wants and send him over to you."

"Be careful," Barrett warned him before Daniel ended the call.

Daniel glanced behind him, no doubt to make sure that she wouldn't be in Rizzo's line of sight, and he paused the security system so he could open the door. Only a fraction, though.

"What do you want?" Daniel snarled.

"A truce," Rizzo said.

She couldn't see either of their faces to gauge their reactions, but Kara was betting that Daniel looked both skeptical and riled. "A truce?" Daniel questioning.

Rizzo huffed. "I'm tired of getting hauled into the sheriff's office for questioning. Tired of you and your brothers hounding me."

Daniel stayed quiet a moment, but Kara figured he was glaring. "You're getting hauled in for questioning because you're a person of interest in an investigation."

She believed Daniel meant the militia case, but Rizzo might not know that Barrett wanted to question him about Daisy's murder and the deaths of the other surrogates and Loretta.

"Yeah, I got that," Rizzo said. "That's why I want a truce. If you really believe I shot somebody, then you'll want to test me for GSR. I'll agree to it. You can test me today."

"Why the change of heart?" The skepticism was still there.

"I just want to have some peace. And FYI, I didn't tamper with the fence your livestock broke through."

Daniel made a sound that could have meant anything. It definitely didn't confirm that he believed Rizzo, and he checked his watch with what no one could mistake as anything but impatience.

"We aren't going to settle our differences here on the porch of the inn," Daniel finally said. "The investigation has to play out. You'll have to be interviewed. After the killer is caught and the Rangers have finished looking into the militia, we'll talk about that truce."

"Killer?" Rizzo questioned. "You mean the woman who was gunned down today?"

"The woman who was gunned down very close to your ranch," Daniel supplied.

Now Rizzo cursed. "You're looking at me for that?" He didn't wait for Daniel to confirm it. "If I was guilty, I would have come up with at least a half-assed alibi and wouldn't have killed her around my own stomping grounds."

"Maybe. But perhaps by setting yourself up like this, you thought it would make you look innocent."

There was more silence before Rizzo grumbled something she didn't catch, and he walked away. Or rather he stormed away, his boots thudding on the porch steps as he left.

Daniel relocked the door, reengaged the security system and went to the window to watch Rizzo leave. He didn't have to say that he didn't trust the man. Neither did she. But Kara thought that Daniel was considering some stronger measures to make sure Rizzo or any of their other suspects didn't come back here.

"The security cameras worked," she said

when she thought Daniel was about to launch into an argument of why they should move. "We're less than a minute away from the sheriff's office. Short of sleeping in the break room there, this is about as safe as it can get for us."

"I considered the break room," Daniel admitted after he huffed. "I'm still considering it."

She wanted to go to him and pull him into her arms. Maybe to try to give him some comfort as he'd done for her. Unfortunately, holding him wouldn't just give comfort, though. It would almost certainly stir the heat along with causing him to worry that she was too close to a window. Instead, she was about to tell him that she would go to the sheriff's office break room if that would make him breathe easier, but his phone rang before she could say anything.

"Barrett," he relayed before putting the call on speaker.

"Rizzo just walked in so I'm guessing everything is okay. What'd he want?"

"A truce. Or so he said," Daniel added with a slathering of skepticism. "He could have been scoping out the place to see what kind of security we have."

Barrett made a sound of agreement. "I'll

bring that up during the interview. He's going to have to wait, though. Eldon's here, and I'm taking him in next."

"You're finished with Sean?" Daniel asked.

"For now. Sean's still with his lawyer in the break room, but I'm going to have to cut him loose. Mason Ryland confirmed his alibi. They were on the phone about the time Daisy was dying. That doesn't mean Sean didn't hire someone to kill her, though."

No, it didn't. And it sickened Kara just to consider that possibility. The possibility that Sean hated her so much that he would murder innocent women in an attempt to cover up the real murders he wanted—Daniel's and hers.

"By the way, Eldon asked to see both of you," Barrett went on. "I told him you'd be watching the interview but that you wouldn't be in the building."

"Do you think it'd help if we were there?" Kara asked.

"No. Because it'd mean you going outside. I know it's not far, but I'd rather you stay indoors with Daniel until we get a better handle on all of this."

A handle on this wouldn't happen until they had the killer behind bars. Right now, Barrett had all three of their suspects in the sheriff's office, but it didn't feel as if they were any closer to putting an end to the danger.

"I'm in my office right now finishing up some paperwork, but I'll be starting Eldon's interview in about ten minutes," Barrett added a moment later. "Text me any questions you want me to ask him."

When Daniel ended the call, he rechecked the locks and security system before he led her back upstairs. No doubt so they could watch the interview with Eldon. They did indeed go straight to the laptop, but Daniel took out his phone to text Leo.

"How's Sadie?" Daniel texted.

Kara certainly hadn't put her worries about the little girl on the back burner, but when Leo didn't immediately respond, it sent the fear skyrocketing. Her frantic mind was already coming up with worst-case scenarios when Daniel's phone dinged. Not with a message but rather a photo.

Of a smiling Sadie.

She was snuggled in Noreen lap while the nanny read her a book. Obviously, Sadie wasn't the least bit worried about being in danger, and Kara was beyond thankful for it. Seeing her, though, was a reminder of just how much Kara missed her. Of course, Daniel felt the same, and she saw the emotions shade his eyes as he ran his finger over the image of his daughter's face.

"She has to stay safe," Daniel muttered, and he sent a thank-you text back to his brother.

"She will." Kara had to believe that because it was the only way she could stay sane.

To get his mind off Sadie, Kara took him by the hand and led him across the room to the laptop. The camera was still on in the interview room, but Daniel had turned off their audio. Probably so that someone in the sheriff's office wouldn't be able to overhear them. However, the audio to the room was still on so they'd be able to listen to Eldon's interview.

As Daniel and she were watching, Esther Ridley, one of the other deputies, escorted Eldon in. Unlike Sean, he didn't have a lawyer with him, but he did immediately look up at the camera.

"Deputy Daniel Logan," the man said, knowing they were watching. "Kara Holland. I needed to talk to you, but the sheriff said you wouldn't be coming in. There are some things you need to know."

Kara glanced at Daniel to get his take on that, but he only shrugged and pinned his attention to the screen. She did the same as Eldon took out an envelope from his pocket.

"Somebody sent me some pictures," Eldon said, speaking directly into the camera. His eyes were narrowed when he pulled out a photo and held it up for them to see.

Kara cursed when she saw the image of the first murdered surrogate, Brenda McGill. It didn't appear to be a crime-scene photo, either. No. In this one, Brenda was sprawled on the floor, face up, her limbs outstretched. The camera had focused on her blank dead eyes.

Oh, God.

Kara's stomach tightened when she realized this could have been taken by the killer.

Daniel hit the button to allow them audio into the room. "Where'd you get that picture?" he demanded while he texted Barrett. He was letting his brother know what was going on.

"Like I said, somebody sent it to me," Eldon insisted. "It came in the mail yesterday. Then, today I got another two."

He took out a second picture, and Kara instantly recognized it, too. It was Mandy Vera, the surrogate who'd been left at Kara's house. This was a shot of Mandy on the bed, right where Daniel and she had found the body.

There was the sound of hurried footsteps,

and Barrett came rushing into the room. He glanced at the picture Eldon was still holding up and then at the camera.

"I was just telling your brother and the surrogate he used that somebody's been sending me pictures," Eldon explained, already reaching for the third one. He said the word *surrogate* like it was vulgar.

Barrett had the same reaction that Daniel and she had. He cursed when he saw Mandy's lifeless body. "I'm taking those into evidence," Barrett insisted.

Eldon nodded as if that'd been exactly what he had expected the sheriff to say. "I just wanted your brother to see this last one." He didn't wait for permission. Eldon just held up the third picture.

It was a darker shot than the other two, but Kara could still see the bed. The same bed where they'd found Mandy. But it wasn't Mandy this time.

Kara gasped before she could stop herself.

Because the person lying on the bed was her.

DANIEL FELT THE punch of fear and dread and figured it was a drop in the bucket compared to what Kara was feeling right now. She had gone pale, and her bottom lip quivered as she stared at the image of herself.

Kara shuddered. "Someone broke into my house and took that picture of me when I was sleeping," she said in a hoarse whisper. "God, when I was in bed and sleeping."

"Maybe. Or it could be Photoshopped." But Daniel didn't really believe that.

Judging from the way she frantically shook her head, neither did Kara. For a good reason. The killer had gotten into her house to leave Mandy's body so it wasn't much of a stretch for him to have broken in another time.

Hell.

He thought of all the times Sadie had been there with Kara. The killer could have gone after them then. He could have taken them both. Hurt them. Or worse.

"This note was clipped to Kara's picture," Eldon went on. He held that up, too, for them, and Daniel had no trouble reading the two words that someone had scrawled on the paper.

She's next.

"The next to die," Kara muttered, dragging in a long breath.

"I'm turning off our audio," Daniel told his brother, and he hit the button to mute the sound from their side. He definitely didn't want Eldon listening in case Kara fell apart. And he thought she might do just that.

Daniel pulled her into his arms and would have kissed her if he thought it would help. It wouldn't. Even the scalding heat between them wasn't going to fix this. The killer—and Eldon—had just shaken her to the core.

"I can't go back to that house," she said, her voice as shaky as the rest of her. "I can't go back home."

That wasn't a surprise. The creep factor was high on this. Especially high, considering that the killer could have murdered her in her sleep.

So, why hadn't he?

If Kara was the target, why hadn't he ended her life then and there?

It was definitely something that Daniel needed to give more thought to, and he could talk that through with Kara. Not now, though. Not while she was trembling in his arms. But soon, the same question would come to her, too. So would the full impact that she'd essentially lost her home. She loved that placed, loved raising and training her horses. It wasn't going to be an easy gap to fill, and while she might change her mind about returning, that would take some time.

"I'm okay," she said several moments later.

It was a Texas-sized lie, but Daniel didn't call her on it. He just kept holding her while he kept watch on the screen as his brother bagged the photos that he took from Eldon.

Eldon looked straight into the camera again. "I figure this sort of thing can mess with a person's head. Of course, I'm figuring her head was already messed up for her to do what she did. Being a surrogate, I mean. People pay in all kinds of ways for the mistakes they make."

That sounded like a veiled threat, but Daniel had to concede that almost anything the man said could be taken that way. After all, Eldon was a suspect, and his showing Kara the pictures could be just part of his cat-and-mouse game.

"I'm having Mr. Shroud wait in my office so I can bag and tag these pictures," Barrett said for Daniel and Kara's benefit. His brother probably didn't want Eldon to have any other chances to take a poke at Kara. "I'll have Esther do the interview with him while I talk to Rizzo. Give me a minute and I'll call to explain what's going on."

Daniel knew it was going to take more than a minute to soothe Kara's jangled nerves. If Eldon had set out to torment her with what he'd shown them, then he'd done a damn good job of it.

"I didn't see any signs of a break-in at my house," she went on, her words and breath hitting against his shoulder and neck. "But it must have happened." He felt her muscles go stiff. "Why?"

He didn't have the answer to that, and Daniel was worried that he might not have it soon enough. As long as the killer was out there, Kara and he wouldn't have any peace. And the child they both loved wouldn't be safe.

Daniel had to put that thought aside when his phone rang. He shifted a little, just enough to answer it, but he kept his arm around Kara. As expected, it was Barrett, and since she was close enough to hear, he didn't put the call on speaker.

"I'll have the photos that I got from Eldon sent to the crime lab," Barrett explained. "He claims he has no idea who sent them."

Daniel jumped right on that. "You believe him?"

His brother sighed. "I just don't know. He's angry all the way to the marrow about his daughter's death so some of that comes through with everything he says. Maybe that's coloring the way I see him."

Daniel was worried the same thing was happening to him. He needed to stay objective because that was the only way to get to the truth.

"The envelopes with the pictures have a San Antonio postmark," Barrett went on. "Eldon admits he's had them in his pocket since they arrived so I suspect any trace will be compromised."

Yeah, so did Daniel, and he was betting that if Eldon wasn't the killer, then the real killer's prints wouldn't be on the envelopes. But that led to an interesting thought.

"Both Sean and Eldon got some kind of correspondence from the killer," Daniel pointed out. "Rizzo didn't."

Of course, that didn't mean Rizzo was guilty. It was just puzzling why he was the only one of their suspects who hadn't gotten that. Then again, the killer might not be either of the three. All three men could be innocent, and if so, that meant Daniel had no idea who was behind these murders and attacks.

"Is Sean still there?" Daniel asked his brother. He might not be able to pin anything on Sean, but he still wanted to keep tabs on him.

"No. He left with his lawyer about ten minutes ago. I got a court order on the financials for all three men, and the files just came through. I'll be looking through those and will go over the interview statements once they're done. I'll send those to you so you can do the same."

Daniel would indeed look over them. Heck, he'd dig through them, looking for any inconsistencies. Since Barrett would be tied up with the interviews and the aftermath of paperwork that would follow those, Daniel appreciated the tasks. It might help him keep his mind off Sadie. Off Kara, too.

Though that'd be harder to do since she was right next to him.

"How'd you manage to get financials on Rizzo?" Daniel asked.

"Leo. He's been working on that from the safe house, and he cited the latest murder and the attack on Kara and you to expedite us getting the files. He'll also deal with putting some pressure on the crime lab and the ME reports. We need to find out if the killer left any piece of himself at Kara's or the clinic when he killed Loretta."

That would be a break if they did find something, but Daniel figured this killer was too smart for that. Still, mistakes happened, and all it took was one hair or one print to blow this investigation wide open.

Barrett didn't waste any time. Within seconds after he ended the call, the financial files on all three suspects came through. Daniel considered going downstairs to the office to print out copies for Kara to read through, but there was a huge window in there, and it was on the ground floor. He preferred to keep her upstairs. Not that a gunman couldn't fire into this room, too, but Daniel had purposely kept her angled away from the single window so as to not give an attacker a direct shot.

He opened the files on his phone, motioning for Kara to take the laptop so she could start reading. "You take Sean's," he said. "I'll start with Rizzo's. Look for any lump sum withdrawals or checks that could have been used to hire a gunman."

She nodded in agreement and got started. Daniel pulled up a chair across from her, and he dug in. He immediately noticed that this was not just Rizzo's financials, but the file also included the notes from the investigation that the Texas Rangers were conducting. The Rangers had highlighted several large online deposits that had been followed with equal withdrawals less than twenty-four hours later.

None in the past couple of days, though.

These were from at least three months ago, shortly before Daniel had gotten that anonymous tip about Rizzo being part of the militia. There wasn't a large withdrawal or deposit after that.

Did that mean Rizzo had just gotten more careful?

Maybe, but he sure as heck hadn't been before then, and Daniel zoomed in on the pattern that the Rangers were obviously trying to establish. Rizzo was getting deposits from a dummy company. Or rather dummy *companies*. Ones that existed only long enough to make the deposits to Rizzo. Then Rizzo was withdrawing the funds, which would have given him cash.

What Daniel was seeing was a way for Rizzo to launder money or to feed that cash from suspicious sources into the militia—maybe for purchasing those weapons they were stockpiling. It wasn't absolute proof that Rizzo was involved in the militia, but it was grounds to hold the man until Daniel and Barrett could take a harder look.

Daniel took out his phone to call his brother, but it rang before he even had a chance to press the number. And it was Barrett.

"You need to hold Rizzo," Daniel immediately told him. "There are red flags in his financials."

Barrett paused as if he were rethinking what he'd been about to say. "I will, but for now I have a problem. I need someone to get to the hospital."

"The hospital?" Kara and Daniel said in unison. Obviously, she'd heard what his brother had said. "What's wrong?"

"Sean's in the ER," Barrett answered. Then he paused and cursed. "Sean claims that you just tried to kill him."

Chapter Thirteen

Kara wasn't sure who looked more stunned about what Barrett had just told them. Daniel or her. Judging from his tone, Barrett was experiencing the same thing.

"Someone tried to kill Sean," Daniel repeated. "How? When? How bad is he hurt?"

"Not sure of any of that yet," Barrett answered. "But he must not be hurt too bad because he just phoned from the ER and wanted me to get there ASAP."

Daniel grumbled some profanity. "Well, it sure as hell wasn't me who tried to kill him. I've been here in the inn with Kara."

"I know that, but I don't know why he said you did. That's why he wanted me up there right now. But I can't go. I have both Rizzo and Eldon in the building, and I don't want to leave Esther here without backup. At the moment, there's no one else I can call in so I'll reschedule the interviews—"

"No." Daniel drew in a long breath and looked at her as if apologizing.

But it wasn't necessary. Kara knew what had to be done. "The hospital is two blocks from here," she reminded Daniel and Barrett. "We can drive there in the cruiser and talk to Sean. We'll try to get to the bottom of what happened."

"I hate to ask," Barrett said a moment later. "But if someone really did try to kill him, we need to know."

"Agreed," Daniel said. "Kara and I will be at the hospital in a couple of minutes."

However, Daniel didn't budge when he ended the call and put away his phone. He did curse some more. And she saw the apology in his eyes as he looked down at her.

"Don't." She pressed a quick kiss on his mouth and holstered her weapon in the back of her jeans. "We'll be careful."

Of course, being careful was no guarantee that they'd be safe since the killer could have set all of this up as a way of luring them out. But the alternative was leaving a deputy alone with two suspects, and Kara didn't want Esther being put at undue risk or having the investigation stall because Barrett couldn't finish the interviews.

"Besides," she added, "both Eldon and Rizzo are in the sheriff's office. Neither of them will be able to fire shots at us."

After several long moments, Daniel finally nodded, and he got them started out of the room and down the stairs. He had to temporarily disengage the security system to get them out the back door, but once they were on the porch, they hurried.

And held their breaths.

Because they both knew that while their suspects wouldn't be able to shoot them at this exact moment, it didn't mean that one of them hadn't hired a henchman or two to do that job.

Kara's heart was pounding by the time they made it into the cruiser. She still held her breath until the doors were shut and Daniel was driving away from the inn. They both fired glances around them, but Kara didn't see anything out of the ordinary. She hoped it stayed that way.

It took less than a minute for them to pull into the hospital parking lot, and Daniel stopped the cruiser as close to the ER doors as he could get. With their hands on their weapons, they hurried inside. A nurse, Gayla Hayward, was right there waiting for them, and she motioned for them to follow her.

"Barrett called me and said you were on your way," Gayla explained. "We have Sean back here in the examining room."

So he wasn't in surgery or intensive care. That was good because he might be able to answer some questions. Especially one question—why he'd accused Daniel of trying to kill him.

"What's Sean's condition?" Daniel asked.

"He has a gunshot wound to the shoulder. Dr. Tipton is with him now."

Kara knew Dr. Norris Tipton since he'd lived in Mercy Ridge his entire life. It was the same for Gayla.

Gayla threaded them through the ER waiting area and down the hall. The moment they stepped into the examination room, Kara spotted Sean. He was lying on the table, and the right side of his shirt was soaked with blood. He immediately sat up, practically snapping to attention, and he aimed fiery narrowed eyes at Daniel.

"You stay the hell away from me," Sean snarled, practically pushing the doctor away so he could try to stand. "I won't let you shoot me again."

"I didn't shoot you," Daniel snarled right back, and he went closer. Like Kara, he examined the wound that Dr. Tipton was cleaning. "How bad is it?"

Dr. Tipton gave Daniel a somewhat annoyed glance, probably because he didn't appreciate being interrupted during an exam. "He'll live," the doctor said. "But he'll need stitches, and I want an X-ray just to be sure."

"Could he have done this to himself?" Daniel pressed, causing a howl of outrage from Sean.

"You tried to kill me," Sean insisted.

Daniel shifted his hard gaze to Sean. "No, I didn't. Tell me what makes you think I did."

"Because I saw your badge. The sun glinted off it just as you shot me."

"You claim you actually saw me pull the trigger?" Daniel snarled. "Or did you just see someone with a badge?"

Sean opened his mouth, closed it, and he cursed before he lay back on the examining table. "I saw the badge. But the shooter was about your size and was wearing a black Stetson like you always do."

She heard Daniel release his breath. "So it could have been someone hired to make you believe it was me."

It seemed to be the last thing Sean wanted to do, but he finally gave a conceding nod that it could have happened that way. "Someone shot me," he growled. "Someone tried to kill me."

Daniel shifted back to the doctor. "Could this wound have been self-inflicted?" he repeated, causing Sean to snarl out another protest.

"Not likely," the doctor commented. "The angle's wrong, and there's no stippling. Have a look for yourself." He moved back so that Daniel could see Sean's injured shoulder.

Stippling was gunshot residue that showed on the skin when the bullet was fired at close range. Which a self-inflicted wound would have been. Kara had a look for herself, and she didn't see any gunshot residue on Sean.

"Satisfied?" Dr. Tipton asked, but he didn't wait for Daniel to answer before he added, "Because I need to finish cleaning this wound, and it's best if Kara and you aren't in here for that."

Daniel volleyed glances between the doctor and Sean, but he didn't budge.

Dr. Tipton sighed. "You can wait in my office. We can chat after I'm finished here."

Daniel finally nodded and tipped his head

to Sean. "He doesn't leave this area until after we've spoken, understand?"

Both the nurse and doctor made sounds of agreement, and Daniel took Kara out of the room and down the hall to Dr. Tipton's office. It wasn't big, just a cluttered desk with two visitors' chairs. And a large window. Daniel immediately went to it and lowered the blinds after he checked to make sure no one was lurking around outside. He took up guard duty at the door that he partially closed but motioned for her to stay back.

"You think Sean had something to do with his own attack?" Kara asked. "That maybe he set this up to make himself look innocent?"

"Maybe." But there was plenty of room for doubt in his tone.

It did seem extreme since Sean had indeed been shot. A shoulder wound could have been serious had the gunman missed just a little, and the bullet could have gone into Sean's neck. So if Sean had hired this guy, he must have had plenty of faith in his abilities.

Since there was no way Kara could sit, she started to pace. Not easy to do in the small space, and of course, she ended up near Daniel. She placed a hand on his arm, causing him to look at her. Their gazes locked. And held. Until Daniel cursed under his breath.

"I'd hoped this would be over," he said.

She thought he was talking about the danger and not the sizzle of attraction that she felt slide between them. Despite their situation, she smiled. "As long as we keep kissing, I don't think it'll be over."

He sure didn't smile. Daniel looked as if he wanted to glare or curse some more. However, he let out a long sigh, and as if resigned to whatever he was feeling for her, he brushed a kiss on her cheek.

Then her mouth.

It might have been barely a touch, but she felt it all right. Mercy, did she. The heat went all the way to her toes, and her body started to rev up for something it wasn't going to get. At least not right now. She couldn't have Daniel, but Kara had no doubts that soon they'd be lovers. They'd no longer be able to resist this hard pull between them, and they'd land in bed. Maybe whatever happened wouldn't destroy the fragile friendship they'd built for Sadie's sake. Maybe they wouldn't ruin everything.

"I just have to focus on keeping you safe," Daniel said as if talking to himself.

She nodded. "I have to focus on keeping you safe, too."

Now he did smile, and Kara wanted to hold on to that moment. She needed it as much as she needed him. But it didn't last because the sound of Daniel's phone shot through the room, and she saw Barrett's name on the screen.

Daniel answered it on speaker, but he put the phone in his shirt pocket. Probably so he could keep his shooting hand free.

"How's Sean?" Barrett immediately asked.

"Alive. But he's injured," Daniel added. "A gunshot wound to the shoulder. I'm waiting on a report from the doctor."

"Good." But Barrett's tone didn't indicate anything good. It was said almost absently as if it was something to check off an important to-do list. "I'm going to have to let Rizzo go."

Daniel groaned. "No. Take a look at the financials. I think he's laundering money for the militia group."

"I did glance over that, and I'll study it more, but lawyers pressed for his release. There's an emergency at his ranch. Someone set several of his barns and outbuildings on fire. The fire department is on the way there now, but the early reports aren't good. There's damage, and the fire's spreading. It could reach some of his livestock, even his house."

"Damage that Rizzo could have caused so that he wouldn't be arrested," Daniel quickly pointed out.

"Maybe." But Barrett didn't sound at all convinced of that. "Sean's been shot, and now this happens on Rizzo's ranch. The only one who hasn't taken any hits is Eldon."

True, but that didn't make the man guilty. Or innocent.

"Anyway, I've let Rizzo go," Barrett went on. "And no, I don't like it any more than you do, but if he tries to run, then it'll only add more weight to his involvement in the militia. That weight, though, doesn't link him to the murders or the attacks, and you know it."

Yes, Daniel did know it, and that's why his next round of profanity was from pure frustration. They probably had enough to get an arrest warrant for Rizzo, but if they wanted to prove he was a killer, they had a long way to go.

Kara didn't especially want to put a positive spin on this, but she had to latch onto some hope. Hope that Rizzo would say or do something to incriminate himself. If not Rizzo, then perhaps Eldon or Sean would do that.

"I just let Eldon go, too," Barrett continued

a moment later. "Since both Rizzo and he will be out on the street, I want Kara and you to go back to the inn ASAP. I can send Esther to the hospital to get the report about Sean from the doctor."

Again, Daniel stayed quiet a moment as if deciding if that was what he should do. He probably wanted to stay put and see if he could get any proof that Sean had orchestrated his own attack. However, her safety must have trumped that option.

"Okay," Daniel finally said. "I'll text you when we get back to the inn."

He ended the call and laid his hand back over his weapon. Kara did the same when he gave her the nod to get them moving. Daniel stepped out into the hall first, glancing around as if he expected someone to jump out and attack them. Kara did the same, but the only person she saw was a nurse.

The hospital wasn't huge by anyone's standards, and this section didn't have actual hospital rooms. It was mainly offices for the doctors, examining rooms for ER patients and the waiting area. That's where they headed, passing by the room where they'd last seen Sean and Dr. Tipton. Kara had hoped the door would be open just so she could get a peek at what was going on, but it was closed.

There was a woman holding a crying baby in the waiting room and another woman at the reception desk. Kara knew both of them. The woman with the baby was Shelby Monroe, and the receptionist was Heidi Coltrane, and she gave them nods of greeting as Daniel and she made their way to the cruiser. However, when they were still about ten feet from the ER doors, she saw something she didn't like.

Smoke.

It was billowing right at the door, seeping in, and it only took her a moment to realize that it was some kind of tear gas or pepper spray. Kara's eyes immediately started to sting, and she began coughing. So did Daniel and the others in the waiting area.

Oh, mercy.

Were they under attack?

Had someone done this so they could try to kill them?

"Run," Daniel snapped to the other women.

Shelby was already doing that. Coughing, she clutched the infant to her chest and began running away from the smoke and into the hall where Daniel and Kara had just been. The receptionist did the same, and Daniel and Kara were right on their heels.

Daniel drew his gun on the run, and he glanced behind them. Just as Kara heard another sound. A hissing sound as if someone had struck a very large match. She looked, but it was impossible to see through the thick smoke. Or at least it was until the flames shot up.

Her heart went to her knees.

Someone had started a fire.

Because she could hardly see and couldn't smell anything other than the tear gas, she couldn't tell if there was some kind of accelerant. It was possible the fire would spread fast, and if that happened, people could be hurt.

Dr. Tipton must have heard the running because he opened the examining room door. His eyes widened when he saw what was going on, but like Kara and the others, he began coughing.

"Get Sean and your nurse out of here," Daniel ordered.

The nurse already had Sean in a wheelchair, and both she and the doctor took hold of it to start hurrying down the hall. But the smoke and the tear gas just kept coming at them. It kept choking them. Making it hard to escape.

Which was no doubt what the killer had planned.

He could be making his way through that smoke and gas right now while he wore a mask. He could be coming to kill them.

"Who the hell did this?" Sean snarled.

No one answered him. Probably because no one knew. Well, unless Sean was the person responsible. He could have hired someone to do this, but if so, he'd put himself right in the mix. If a gunman started shooting now, he could hit Sean or any of the rest of them. Including that baby.

That sent a spike of raw anger through Kara. How dare this snake do something to put an innocent child in danger.

Ahead of them, Shelby, who still had her arms wrapped around her baby, stumbled, and Kara didn't know how Daniel managed it, but he sprang toward her, catching them before they could fall.

"Kara, keep watch behind us," Daniel told her, and she tried, but it was impossible to see anything.

Overhead, the sprinklers made a hissing sound a split second before the cold water began spewing down on them. That would help put out the fire. At least Kara prayed it would.

But at the moment it was making it even harder for her to see.

"Don't go in there," Daniel said when Dr. Tipton reached for one of the office doors.

Kara knew why Daniel had said that. He didn't want the doctor to go into a room where he could be trapped by the fire. The fire department was almost certainly on the way, but it only took seconds to be overcome by the smoke and flames.

They all kept running, with others joining them, but Daniel stopped when they reached the back exit. He opened the door but motioned for them to stay back.

Because a killer could be out there.

Waiting.

Ready to strike.

And suddenly the stakes were so much higher now that there were so many people who could be gunned down. Kara remembered the wild, almost random shots that'd been fired at Daisy when she'd been running in the pasture. If that happened now, the baby could be hurt.

Even though the water from the sprinkler was getting into Kara's eyes, it helped some with washing away the burning that the gas and smoke had caused. It must have done the same thing for Daniel because he seemed to focus when he looked outside. Then he turned his gaze to her.

"You'll have to cover me while I get them out," he said.

She didn't have to ask who he meant by *them*—Shelby and her child. Kara nodded and stepped into the doorway to watch for a gunman while Daniel hooked his left arm around the woman. He whisked them out of the hospital and hurried them to a car several yards away. He had them get down on the ground and then under the vehicle before he motioned for the doctor to bring out Sean. However, before Dr. Tipton could do that, there was the sound of a blast.

Someone had fired a shot.

Kara couldn't tell what the bullet had hit. She prayed it wasn't Daniel, Shelby or the baby. But she caught onto the doctor to hold him back. It wasn't easy. Because they were all still fighting for their breaths, the instinct was to run. To get out in the fresh air, but that could be a fatal mistake.

She moved ahead of the doctor and Sean, and despite the clogged air, Sean still managed to growl out some profanity. Kara pushed the sound of his voice aside and kept watch. She listened. She heard the howl of sirens, probably both the fire department and Barrett.

There were other voices coming from other parts of the hospital. Shouts for people to evacuate. Which they would almost certainly do. And they might run straight into gunfire.

Kara lifted her head, listening for any sign of the shooter. From the front end of the car, she spotted Daniel doing the same thing. Their eyes met, and it seemed for a second that time froze.

Then a second shot came.

This one smacked into the door just inches from where Kara was standing. She automatically ducked back in, shoving the doctor and Sean farther into the hall and against the wall. She waited, holding her breath and listening for the next shot.

She didn't have to wait long.

This one tore through the front of the car, close to where Daniel had crouched, and Kara risked looking out to see if she could spot the gunman. Thanks to the smoke, she couldn't, and she didn't think this particular smoke was coming from the fire at the front of the building. She thought that maybe their attacker had set off some kind of device to give him cover.

And it was working.

Kara couldn't see him, and she couldn't just fire in his general direction because she might hit an innocent bystander. But she had to do something. As long as there was gunfire, the fire department wouldn't be able to come onto the scene. The hospital could be severely damaged, and there were likely plenty of people still inside.

Instead of aiming at the gunman, Kara lifted her weapon and fired into the sky. It was still a risk since she could hit a power line, but at the moment anything they did carried huge risks. She fired a second shot. Then waited.

It didn't take her long to pick through the other sounds and hear something. Footsteps.

Someone was running. And she didn't have to guess who.

The shooter was getting away.

Chapter Fourteen

Using the binoculars that he'd taken from the cruiser, Daniel stood at the second-floor window of the inn and watched the chaos still going on around the hospital.

Since the sun had already set, it was dark, but the lights on the tall poles in the parking lot still gave him enough illumination to see the scene well enough. The fire department had managed to put out the flames, and everyone had been evacuated from the building itself.

That was the good news.

But the parking lot was a sea of emergency vehicles, first responders and even some patients who were being treated for smoke inhalation and other injuries. They'd gotten damn lucky with the assortment of injuries. None of them had been serious, and that was nothing less than a miracle. It could have been so much worse.

Daniel hated that he couldn't be there to help, but there was no way he could keep Kara on the scene once other law enforcement had come in. Especially since Kara and he were almost certainly the targets of the attack. If they'd stuck around, it would have continued to put others in danger.

That definitely wasn't a comforting thought.

Neither was the fact that despite the latest incident, they still weren't close to making an arrest and putting an end to this exile. Not just for Kara and him but also for Sadie.

He heard the shower turn off and knew that Kara would soon be coming out of the bathroom. Daniel tried to steel himself up and get some of the worry off his face. No need for her to see that on him since she was no doubt feeling plenty of it herself.

This attack had shaken her even more than the other ones. He had felt that when he was finally able to lead her away from the scene. They'd walked out, literally having to step around those getting medical treatment, and Kara was almost certainly blaming herself for what'd happened. It wasn't her fault. Hell, it wasn't his, either.

But it sure felt like it was.

Wearing the bathrobe that she had tightly

cinched around her, Kara stepped from the bathroom, her gaze immediately going to his. "Anything new on the gunman?" she asked.

Though she probably already knew the answer to that, Daniel shook his head. "But I did get a call from Barrett just a couple of minutes ago. He said it looks as if both the tear gas and the incendiary device that caused the fire were on timers. They were tucked behind concrete plant holders just inside the ER doors."

She stayed quiet a moment, her forehead bunched up while she obviously gave that some thought. "I'm guessing the security camera didn't catch who put the device and tear gas there?"

Daniel had to shake his head again. "The only cameras are in the areas where meds are stored."

That wasn't out of the ordinary for a small town hospital in an area with a very low crime rate. Still, he wished there'd been just one camera to catch whoever had done this. Of course, if there had been, their attacker might have been able to disarm any security.

"A timer means we can't rule out any of our suspects," she added a moment later. She sighed, pushed her damp hair from her face and walked toward him to join him at the window.

Bingo. That's exactly what it meant. Added to that, there might not have even been a hired gun if the attacker was Eldon or Rizzo. Both men had time to get to the hospital after leaving the sheriff's office.

But Sean was a different matter.

He'd been right there with them, and he certainly hadn't fired any shots. So, maybe he had a henchman helping him. That would explain why the shooter hadn't aimed any bullets in Sean's direction. Then again, if Sean had set the timer, he might not have minded being in the thick of an "escape." Especially if he knew there was no real threat to him. It could have given him some kind of sick thrill to watch them run for their lives.

"We don't have proof yet," he went on, "but it appears that the fires set at Rizzo's ranch were also on timers. He lost two barns, and his back porch was damaged. No injuries, though."

"That's good," she muttered, taking the binoculars from him so that she could look at the hospital. It wasn't a long look, though. Kara only eyed the carnage for a couple of seconds before she sighed again and handed him back the binoculars. "What about Shelby and her baby?"

Here was where he could give her some peace of mind. "Both are okay. Not a scratch on them. They were treated at the scene for smoke inhalation and then released."

"Good," she repeated, sounding a lot more relieved than she had been about the lack of injuries in the fires at Rizzo's place.

Daniel could add to that peace of mind with something else he had to tell her. "Sadie's all right. I called the safe house while you were in the shower. She was already asleep so I didn't get a chance to talk to her, but Leo said she had a fun day."

He welcomed the ghost of a smile that put on Kara's face. He'd had the same reaction, and he wished they could both hang on to it awhile longer. Especially since all the updates he had to give her weren't good news.

"The Rangers are digging through Rizzo's financials," he went on. "But it's possible those deposits and withdrawals are for cattle purchases and sales. The Rangers might not be able to use them to link him to the militia."

That meant they also couldn't use it to arrest Rizzo, which made him a free man. For the time being, anyway. Barrett was still interviewing people who'd been in or around the hospital at the time of the attack. It was possible one of them had seen the person responsible, and maybe that person was Rizzo.

"What about the pictures that Eldon had?" Kara asked. "Are those already at the lab?"

"They are and they'll be processed ASAP since they're connected to a multiple-murder investigation." Now he had to pause and take a deep breath before he gave Kara another dose of bad news. "The San Antonio police found Marissa Rucker's body."

No need to explain who Marissa Rucker was. Kara knew that she'd been a surrogate. The very one who'd also used the Willingham Fertility Clinic. And she'd been missing for several days now.

"How'd she die?" Kara's voice hardly had any sound now, and she went way too pale. She suddenly looked ready to face-plant on the floor, so Daniel took hold of her arm to help steady her.

"She'd been shot," he told her.

He didn't intend to mention that she'd also been bashed in the head. There'd been plenty of anger in her attack, but unfortunately not much evidence since the body had been exposed to the elements for at least four days.

Kara nodded as if trying to accept that, but

he knew there was no way she could accept something as senseless as another murder.

"Once SAPD pinpoints Marissa's time of death, they'll want to question our suspects to see if they have alibis." Of course, even if they didn't have them, it still might not lead to an arrest. Everything they had right now was circumstantial.

"Daniel," she whispered. Kara said his name like a weary sigh and moved closer, putting her head against his shoulder.

Even though she'd no doubt done that just for comfort, the closeness set off some alarms inside him. He'd been telling himself to keep his hands off her. Not to let what he was feeling for her interfere with the investigation. But his body didn't care much about alarms.

Daniel set the binoculars aside and slid his arms around her.

She made another of those weary sigh sounds, and the moment crawled by while he just held her. He didn't pull her closer. Didn't kiss her. However, it certainly felt as if that was going on.

And more.

He got some very clear images of stripping off that robe and taking her to the bed that was only a few yards away. But that would be a mistake. Kara wasn't in a good state of mind right now and wasn't ready for something like that.

Or so he thought.

But he had to do a mental adjustment when she eased back enough to locate his mouth with hers. He might have planned on resisting a kiss, but he sure didn't. Her lips felt as if she intended to make this count. To make this ease some of that tension bubbling inside her.

Daniel was all for relieving tension, all for the pleasure that being with her would give them, but he didn't deepen the kiss. He just let her take the lead. And she took it all right. Her tongue ran along the seam of his lips, and Kara went in to take this to a whole different level.

That *different level* went straight to his groin. Man, her taste got to him and made him want a whole lot more. But more wasn't necessarily a good thing. It could turn out to be something Kara would regret, and that's why he had to give her an out.

"You should probably get some rest," he managed to say when she finally broke for air.

She pulled back enough to meet him eye to eye. "Do you really want me to rest?" Kara asked.

Hell. That was a hard question with an easy

answer. No. He wanted her naked and beneath him in the bed. Or on top of him. It didn't matter. He just wanted her, and when Daniel stared down into her eyes, he knew that want was going to win out.

He lowered his head and took her mouth.

KARA HAD FELT Daniel's hesitation. But then she'd also felt that hesitation snap like a twig when the heat took over.

She was thankful he'd lost that particular battle. They'd have to deal with the consequences of this after. But for now, they could be together, and for a little while they could forget the attacks, the murders. The danger. For now, it could be just the two of them and the pleasure they could give each other.

And Kara was certain there would indeed be pleasure.

His scent swirled around her as she sank into his taste. A taste that fueled a wildfire that already had a life of its own. A fire that she was certain would get a whole lot hotter.

The kiss raged on until her mouth felt slightly bruised, and Daniel's strong arm wrapped around her waist, hauling her to him. Not that he had to do much of that. Kara was already against him.

"Kara," he said, whispering her name as he buried his face into her hair.

There was so much emotion in that one word. Both the pleasure and the doubts all mixed with the heat and need. He was worried about this. About her. But that wouldn't stop them. Not with this urgency pushing at them to finish this.

And Daniel got started on the finishing.

He took those lethal kisses to the sensitive spots on her neck. She wasn't sure how he'd known just where to kiss. Where to touch. But he did, and he was very good at it.

Kara tried to kiss him and touch him as well, but everything started to move too fast, and she had to hold on to him to anchor herself. Without stopping that firestorm of kisses, he walked them to the bed. Not gently. Each step seemed to be a battle to milk out every ounce of pleasure. To make and then take even more. Kara very much wanted that more.

The moment her back landed on the soft bed, he shoved open the robe. She was only wearing a bra and panties beneath, and she nearly lost her breath when he skimmed his hot gaze, then his hand, down her body. She hadn't needed anything else to make her want him, but that did it.

Her mouth was so hungry, and she was starved for him when she kissed him. When she got open the buttons on his shirt and touched his chest, she let her fingers trail through the thick mat of dark hair that he had there. Then she kept trailing until she reached his stomach where the muscles tightened under her touch.

His body was perfect, of course. She'd known it would be. She kept touching, kept her hand sliding lower until she pressed her palm over the front of his jeans. He was huge, hard and ready. That, in turn, made her ready as well, and she felt her own heat pool in the center of her body.

He made a husky sound of pleasure that nearly caused her to melt. That sound, the look he gave her, was a potent weapon in his sexual arsenal.

"Now," she insisted.

But Daniel didn't listen. Apparently, he wasn't done with the kissing and touching because he lowered the cups of her bra, and with the lightest touch, he flicked his tongue over her nipples. First one, then the other. He might as well have doused her with carnal fire because that *now* became a lot more urgent.

"Now," she repeated.

He must have taken her at her word because he went after her panties. He kissed her along the way as he pushed them down. Down. Down. Kissing her right between her legs.

Kara heard her own sound of pleasure, and for a moment she nearly gave in to the pleasure he was creating with his mouth and tongue. But she didn't want to do this solo. She wanted Daniel with her when she climaxed.

With her hands shaking from the need, Kara unhooked his belt and would have freed him from his boxers, but he eased her hand away. "Condom," he said.

He might as well have asked for the moon because she lay there, burning. Needing. And knowing that she didn't have a condom. Thankfully, though, Daniel did. He fished out his wallet from his back pocket and took out the foil wrapper.

Clamping the edge of the wrapper between his teeth, he shoved his jeans and boxers past his hips. The moment he had on the condom, he was back on top of her.

And inside her.

This was many steps past mere pleasure with that first thrust. Her breath went wild. Her heart pounded. And she wanted him with every fiber of her being.

He moved. Slowly. So slowly. Which only made the need more frantic. Kara pulled at his hips, thrusting hers up to meet him. She didn't even try to make this last. She couldn't. The fire was way too hot for that, and her body wasn't going to settle for anything less than the fast orgasm that only Daniel could give her.

Finally, the heat must have gotten to him, too, because he started to move faster. Deeper. Thrust after thrust. With her lifting her hips to meet each one.

Until she could take no more.

The climax slammed through her, clamping onto his erection and causing Daniel to slide right over that peak with her. She felt his body give way. Heard the hitch of his breath. As his muscles went slack.

She rode out the pleasure from the aftershocks, keeping her arms wrapped around Daniel. The emotions hit her all at once. The incredible sensations of his weight on her. The way his skin felt against hers. His mouth when he sought out her lips for a lazy, sated kiss.

But what hit her most were the feelings that seemed to pour from her heart.

Feelings that Daniel probably didn't want her to have, but there was no way Kara could stop them. Not now. Not after she'd been with him like this.

She was in love with him.

Chapter Fifteen

Daniel lay in the darkness, staring up at the ceiling while he wondered just how much he'd screwed things up.

The sex with Kara had been great. But then that was no surprise. A scalding heat made for scalding hot sex. However, there could be a huge price to pay for it. Kara knew that, too, and he figured she was having as many doubts as he was.

Well, maybe she was.

Maybe she had such deep feelings for him that this would end up hurting her. Daniel hated that, but he wasn't sure there was a way to avoid it. It didn't feel as if his heart was his to give, that he might not be able to forget Maryanne and move on with his life.

He mentally shook his head, though, rethinking that. The fact that he was here in bed with a naked Kara snuggled against him was perhaps proof that he had moved on. He wasn't sure if that bothered him, but he was certainly having some pangs of guilt over not feeling, well, guilty.

"You can't sleep?" Kara whispered, letting him know that she was well aware he was awake.

"Neither can you?" he countered, looking down at her. And thanks to the night-light coming from the bathroom, he got an eyeful. One that made him want her all over again.

The sheet had dipped down a couple of inches, exposing her left breast, and she had one leg on top of the covers. Her face was as beautiful as it always was. Then there was her mouth. It looked a little swollen from all the kissing they'd done, which only reminded him that kissing her had been darn pleasurable and that he wouldn't mind doing more of it again.

Like now, for instance.

Despite the guilt lecture he'd just given himself, Daniel found himself leaning in to brush a kiss over her lips. She moved closer, sliding right into the kiss, which would have no doubt led to more sex.

If his phone hadn't rung.

Daniel quickly disentangled himself from Kara and snatched up his cell from the nightstand. He saw Barrett's name on the screen and checked the time. Since it was nearly midnight, this couldn't be good news.

Sadie.

That was his first thought, and Daniel blurted out his daughter's name the moment he answered. He added a quick, "Is Sadie okay?"

"She's finc," Barrett assured him, but Daniel could tell from his brother's tone that not all was well.

"What happened?" Daniel snapped. He got up and started to get dressed. Kara did the same.

"One of Rizzo's ranch hands just called," Barrett explained. "Rizzo was supposed to be staying in a guesthouse on the ranch grounds since the main house had some fire damage. The hand heard what he thought might be a gunshot coming from the guesthouse so he went to check it out. Rizzo didn't answer when the hand knocked at the door. When he went in, he said there are signs of a struggle, and that Rizzo's nowhere around."

Daniel released the breath he'd been holding. This didn't sound good for Rizzo, but this didn't have anything to do with Sadie or the rest of his family. At least he hoped it didn't.

"So, Rizzo's missing," Daniel concluded.

"That's what the ranch hand believes. He insists he's checked all around the ranch, and he can't find his boss. He says Rizzo's phone is still in the guesthouse. His wallet, too."

Daniel thought about that for a moment. The phone and wallet weren't good. People didn't normally leave those things behind if they went out.

"Signs of a struggle," Daniel repeated. "Maybe the sound of a gunshot. But no blood?"

"No, but I'm heading out there now to have a look," Barrett answered. "I was at my place so I'm not that far from Rizzo's ranch. I told the hand to get out of the guesthouse in case it's a crime scene. I don't want him mucking up any possible evidence."

Daniel didn't like that at all. This could be some kind of trap to lure Barrett into danger. "Do you have backup?"

"Yeah, Esther's meeting me there. She was off duty, but I called her back in to help with this."

Barrett had had to do that because there weren't many options, not with Leo, Daniel and Cybil all tied up with protection details. The night deputy, Jake Mendoza, would be at the sheriff's office, but he would have to stay in town to be able to respond to any emergencies.

"There's more," Barrett continued several moments later. "The ranch hand said that Rizzo's truck is also missing. If someone kidnapped him, then they might be in the truck."

True. But there was another option. If Rizzo had faked an attack to draw Barrett and other lawmen away from town, then Rizzo could be using his truck to come to the inn. Or escape if he truly believed he was about to be arrested.

"FYI, I just tried to contact Eldon," Barrett said. "I was going to ask him if he knew anything about Rizzo, but mainly I wanted to see if he had an alibi. The call went straight to voice mail."

Since it was late, that wasn't unusual. Some people did turn off their phones at night. But nothing about this felt right. Apparently, his brother felt the same way, and that's why he'd called.

"I just want you to make sure your security system is still activated and that no one set it off," Barrett insisted.

"I'll check that now."

Daniel put on his holster and drew his gun. With Kara doing the same thing and following right behind him, they hurried downstairs. The light on the security monitor was engaged, and there weren't any red lights to indicate an open window or door. Still, they went through the bottom floor to check each one.

"Everything's secure," Daniel relayed. He checked the security app on his phone. "And none of the exterior cameras have been triggered."

Of course, if any of the cameras had been, he would have gotten a signal. Still, Daniel went to the front window and peered out to verify no one was there. He didn't see anyone.

But he saw *something.*

"There's a dark blue truck parked just up the street. I can't make out the license plate, but I think it could be Rizzo's. It's parked just out of range of the security cameras."

Barrett muttered some profanity. "Sit tight, and I'll call Jake to have him check it out."

Since Deputy Mendoza was less than two blocks away, it wouldn't take him long to do that. However, that didn't ease the tight ball of tension that settled in Daniel's gut.

Something was wrong.

And Daniel got confirmation of that just seconds later.

His phone beeped, the sound piercing right through him. Because someone had just triggered one of the security cameras.

KARA TRIED TO steel herself up for the jolt of fear and adrenaline that came. From the moment she'd heard the concerned tone of Barrett's voice, she had thought there might be trouble. She just hadn't considered that trouble might already be waiting for them outside.

"What's wrong?" Barrett asked.

Daniel didn't answer his brother until he'd gone through each of the various screens of the cameras. "I don't see anything, but something or someone tripped the alarm."

Maybe the same someone who'd left Rizzo's truck up the street. Of course, it might not actually be Rizzo. If the ranch hand had indeed heard a shot and Rizzo had been taken by force, then his kidnapper could have brought the truck here and come close enough to set off the sensor on the camera.

"I need to go back upstairs and view the camera feed on the laptop," Daniel told his brother. "If I see anyone, I'll call you back." He ended the call and shoved his phone back in his pocket.

There was only a small light on the reception desk, but Daniel turned it off before they rushed back up the stairs. Kara tried to listen for any indications of someone breaking in. Or another camera alarm triggering. But there was nothing like that. She could only hear the sounds of Daniel's and her hurried footsteps and her own gusting breath.

Just minutes ago, Daniel and she had been in bed. And while she couldn't say they hadn't had a care in the world, the sex had soothed her raw nerves. So had Daniel. Well, there was no soothing now, not until they were certain that they weren't about to be attacked.

Once they were back in the bedroom, Daniel raced to the computer, but Kara went straight to the window. Daniel had warned her enough to stay out of anyone's possible line of sight so she peered out the side of the blinds. She looked past the cruiser parked there, past the sliver of a backyard and into the area that the cameras wouldn't cover.

Still nothing.

Mercy Ridge had very little nightlife so there wasn't anyone out strolling around, but she looked to make sure a cat or some other animal hadn't inadvertently set off the sensor.

"According to the security log, the camera in the eastside yard was the one that went off," Daniel relayed to her.

He motioned for her to follow him, and while balancing his laptop on his forearm, they rushed down the hall to what was called the east room. It was a large suite and had not one but two large windows that faced that particular part of the yard. Kara went to one. Daniel, the other. But just like the back, Kara couldn't see anything that would have tripped it.

"Maybe someone's playing games," she murmured.

A sick game.

The person could have thrown a rock or something at the camera so they'd get the alarm and go into a scramble. But why? If this was the killer, certainly he knew that Daniel and she wouldn't just go running outside to see if there was a threat. Plus, anyone who knew Daniel would also know that he would tell his brother the sheriff about this.

Then again, Barrett wasn't nearby.

He was out at Rizzo's.

Maybe that ploy had been part of this. Something that caused Kara's heart to pound even harder. But she forced herself to remember that there was a deputy at the sheriff's office. They would have backup if needed. And it wasn't as if Daniel and she were defenseless. They were both armed and wouldn't just stand by while someone attacked them.

Daniel's phone dinged again, and the soft sound went through her as effectively as a scream. Her body braced. Her hand tightened on her gun. And with her breath held, she waited while Daniel scanned his laptop screen.

"It's the camera at the back of the inn this time," he snarled.

Unfortunately, they couldn't see that particular spot from these windows so they had to hurry back to the room they'd just left. This time it was Daniel who went to the window, but he kept his attention on the laptop.

And he cursed.

That sent Kara running to him, and she looked around his shoulder, trying to see what had caused that reaction. Nothing. Not at first, anyway. Then she zoomed in on a shadow at the back of the yard. It wasn't out in the open but rather next to a spindly Texas mountain laurel tree.

Maybe a person.

It was hard to tell, so she watched, waiting for some kind of movement. But nothing. Kara was so focused on that one spot that she gasped when the sound of Daniel's phone ringing shot through the room. He passed her the laptop so he could take out his phone and answer it.

"Daniel," Barrett blurted out the moment he was on the line. "Is everything okay there?"

"Someone or something keeps triggering

the cameras. It could be a kid who thinks this is a fun prank."

Judging from Daniel's tone, he didn't believe that. Neither did Kara.

Barrett stayed quiet a couple of moments. "There's blood in the guesthouse where Rizzo was staying, and there appears to be signs of a struggle."

Kara tried to look at that from several angles. Maybe Rizzo had indeed been the victim of a crime. Heck, he could be dead. Then again, he could have orchestrated all of this to make himself look innocent, and at this very minute he could be waiting by that mountain laurel.

But there was no way she could just focus on Rizzo as the culprit. Eldon could have done this. Or even Sean. His shoulder injury might be the real deal, but that wouldn't necessarily stop him from breaking into Rizzo's guesthouse and abducting him at gunpoint.

"I'm calling in a crime scene team," Barrett added a moment later, "and then I'm heading back your direction."

Good. Because Kara had the feeling that Daniel and she were going to need all the help they could get.

Daniel ended the call and went back to his

search for a possible intruder. He slid his cop's gaze from the laptop screen back to the edge of the window. Kara moved, hoping that a slightly different angle would help her get a better look at that shadowy figure, but before she could do that, there was another sound.

A blast.

And the glass from the window came flying at them.

Tossing his laptop aside, Daniel hooked his arm around her waist, pulling her to the floor, but Kara was already heading in that direction. A little too late, though. She felt the shards of glass slice over her face and arms. She felt the sting of the cuts. Felt her blood on her skin.

Felt the fear slam into her.

She turned to make sure Daniel was okay, but she didn't even manage a glimpse of him before there was another shot. Not a bullet this time. But a small metal canister burst through what was left of the window and landed on the floor next to them.

Smoke spewed from it, filling the room.

DANIEL HAD A flashback of the nightmare of the smoke that'd billowed through the hospital. Of Kara and him having to run to safety. Of the shots that'd followed once they'd made it to the parking lot. Even more memories of the bullets that had come within a breath of killing them and the others they'd been trying to get out.

And he braced himself for that to happen again.

At least now they didn't have a baby in the path of those bullets, but Daniel had no doubts that this was going to go from bad to worse in the blink of an eye. Someone could hear the shots and come to try to help. He seriously doubted a killer would just let that happen. No. He'd gun down whoever got in his way because it was obvious whoever was doing this wanted to make sure this was the last attack.

The one that'd leave Kara and him dead.

But who was doing this? Daniel quickly pushed that question aside. It wouldn't help him now because no matter who it was, he had to make sure the person didn't succeed. He couldn't let this SOB kill Kara and anyone else.

"Stay low and start moving," he snapped to Kara, but the anger roiled inside him when he saw her face.

The blood.

Hell, there was so much of it in her hair and on her face that he couldn't tell how serious her injuries were. He wanted to take out the killer for doing this to her. Wanted him to pay and pay hard. But he had to put that on hold and try to get her out of there. No choice about it. The smoke was already starting to smother them.

Regardless of the blood and what had to be pain from her injuries, she started crawling. And despite the coughing, Kara managed to keep hold of her gun. Daniel wasn't sure, however, that she could see well enough to shoot straight.

Each inch they crawled felt like a mile, and he felt the pieces of broken glass dig into his own hands and knees. That didn't stop him, though, because Daniel knew the person who was doing this could continue to send more of that glass raining down on them.

There was another shot, and it ripped into the wall just as they made it into the hall. Daniel quickly reached up and slammed the door shut. A bullet could still go through the wood, but he was hoping to stop some of the smoke from filling up the rest of the house.

Kara sat up, putting her back against the wall while she gulped in some long breaths. Daniel used his shirtsleeve to wipe away some of the blood from her face, but it was too dark to tell if she had any deep gashes. He thought he might have a deep cut of his own on his knee, but he'd have to deal with that later.

It ate up precious seconds, but Daniel took the time to message Barrett to let him know what was going on. "We're under attack," he texted. "Approach with caution. Active shooter in the area."

Maybe that would keep his brother and the other deputies safe. He definitely didn't want them walking into an ambush.

He took hold of Kara's arm and moved her away from the room. Away from the stream of smoke that was already seeping under and around the door. They definitely couldn't just sit there and let the smoke overtake them, but he wasn't sure where he should take her.

And then he caught a whiff of something else.

That "going from bad to worse" had just happened.

"We need to get down the stairs," Daniel told her.

She shook her head, maybe not understanding why he'd said that, but then Kara lifted her head. She sniffed and cursed when she no doubt caught the scent of the accelerant.

Gasoline.

Daniel didn't think the killer had actually

gotten it in the house. Probably the back porch, though. But it would still be enough to burn the place down, especially since the fire department wouldn't be able to respond until they were certain there were no other shots being fired.

He considered going back in the room to get his laptop, but it was too risky. Instead, Daniel had a quick look on his phone to view the feed from the security cameras. The phone screen suddenly seemed way too small, but he saw the fire. Not on the back porch but rather the front one.

There didn't appear to be anyone in the backyard where the cruiser was parked. But, of course, a killer wouldn't just stand out in the open for them to see.

Daniel cursed himself for not having brought any Kevlar vests to the inn. Cursed his plan that had brought Kara here in the first place so all of this could be set in motion.

Now, because of the bad decisions he'd made, he might get her killed.

The realization of that squeezed at his heart, and it sickened him. But Daniel battled back those feelings and got her moving to the stairs. He had to try to get Kara out of there. Later, he could take the time to berate himself.

If there was a later, that is.

Despite the smoke and the fire, Daniel didn't run with her down the stairs. It was pitch dark, and he couldn't risk them falling. Right now, any other injuries could be just as dangerous as the killer's bullets because it could trap them inside.

He didn't know if it was the killer's actual intention to burn the place to the ground, but Daniel couldn't risk staying inside where the smoke could overtake them and leave them unconscious.

Each step was another effort, and despite the darkness, he kept watch. He didn't see anything other than the dark shadows of the furniture, but he could hear plenty. Somewhere in the house, a clock chimed, and the old stairs creaked. And he could hear the crackle of the flames as the fire battered away at the front porch. There was black smoke seeping beneath this door, too.

"This way," he whispered, taking hold of Kara's arm so they wouldn't get separated in the darkness.

Daniel headed to the kitchen, already dreading the wall of windows that he knew was there. There were side exits, two of them, but both of those would put them much farther away from the cruiser. The back door was much closer.

Something that the killer almost certainly knew.

"We'll have to go out there," he heard Kara mutter. It wasn't a question, but it was laced with as much concern as Daniel felt.

"Yeah," he verified. "But we'll take some precautions."

Such that they were. They wouldn't just go running out into the backyard, but they were going to have to get to the cruiser. So that meant using whatever they could for cover.

By the time they reached the kitchen, the smoke had already made it back to this part of the house, and he doubted the front door would hold up much longer. Once it was gone, the fire would begin to make its way throughout the rest of the inn. Daniel didn't know how much time they had before that happened, but he figured they had mere minutes.

With his hold still on Kara, he made sure she didn't go directly in front of the windows. That meant crouching down and heading to the door. Daniel had to turn off the security system—a huge risk since the gunman could sneak inside and ambush them from behind—

but he needed to be able to hear. He couldn't do that with the alarm blaring.

"We crawl out onto the porch," he explained. "Stay behind the railing, and we'll make our way to the steps."

If they managed that without anyone shooting at them, then they could go into the yard.

Kara nodded, and using her forcarm, she swiped away the blood that was trickling into her eyes. She clearly needed medical attention. If he managed to get her into the cruiser, he could take her to the sheriff's office and call the EMTs to come and treat her.

For now, though, they had to leave.

Daniel sent another text to Barrett to let his brother know that Kara and he would be outside, and then he took out the keys to the cruiser, and using the remote function on the keypad, he unlocked it. Next, he unlocked the back door, automatically pulling Kara to the floor with him.

"Let's go," he said after taking a deep breath.

Daniel opened the door and got them moving.

Chapter Sixteen

Kara began to crawl, her bloody palms pressed against the cool wood of first the kitchen floor and then the porch.

She tried to force her hands to stop shaking. It was hard to do because of the fresh slam of adrenaline she'd just gotten, but she had to stay in control. Well, as much control as she could manage, considering she was bleeding in too many places to count and was terrified.

The terror wasn't for herself but rather for Daniel. She knew he would go to any lengths to protect her. Any. Lengths. That would include putting himself between her and any gunfire that'd come their way.

He could end up dying for her.

And she didn't want that. Kara didn't want to leave her niece an orphan, so if it came down to Daniel and her under a killer's bullet, she'd make sure that he wasn't the one to die.

They'd gone only a few inches outside the door when there was another shot. This one blasted into one of the windows, causing more glass to shatter down on them. And worse, the glass now littered the porch, making it even more dangerous for them to keep going.

"Try to get to the railing," Daniel whispered, and as she'd predicted he would do, he levered himself up enough to cover her body with his.

The railing wasn't far, only about six feet away, but Kara was sure she left a bloody trail each time her hands and knees scraped over the wood. Her heart was pounding so hard that it was throbbing in her ears, making it hard to hear. Hard to think, too. Still, she got there and pressed herself against the wrought iron railing.

She wished the railing had been a solid metal sheet. Or any kind of solid material for that matter. But there were several inches of gaps between each of the metal stakes, and that meant Daniel and she could still be easy targets.

Especially Daniel.

He was still looming over her while he fired his gaze all around the yard, but Kara did something about that. She took hold of the front of his shirt and yanked him farther down.

"If he kills you, then I'll be a much easier target," she managed to say.

She knew it was playing dirty to remind Daniel of something like that, but it worked. He cursed. And he stayed down.

The moments crawled by while they both tried to pinpoint the shooter. Tried to pinpoint other sounds, too. There were no wails of sirens, but Kara heard a vehicle approaching the front of the inn. Probably the fire department. A moment later, she got confirmation of that when Daniel got a text.

He didn't take his attention off their surroundings, but instead Daniel passed his phone to her. She saw the text from Barrett.

I'm out front with the firefighters, his brother messaged. We'll hold until I get the green from you.

The green. The go-ahead to let him know it was safe to come to the back of the inn, safe for the firemen to get out of their vehicle and fight the blaze. But neither of those things might happen.

What's your location? Barrett texted.

It took some doing because of the blood on her hands, but Kara answered, On the back porch.

She would have added that they were under

fire, but there was no need for her to do that. At that exact moment, two more shots came. These came from the back left side of the yard, and both bullets slammed into the window, bringing down yet more glass. Once again, Daniel covered her, his back taking the falling shards.

The anger came, as hot as the fire that slimy snake had set. Whoever was doing this was trying to rip Daniel and her to shreds, and they couldn't just lay there and let it happen. Plus, if the fire wasn't contained soon, it could spread to other buildings. People could be hurt. Or worse.

"I'll fire over his head," she whispered. That way, she wouldn't hit any bystanders. "He might run again."

Daniel made a sound to let her know he wasn't convinced that would happen, but he shifted, levering himself up again. "I'll do it."

And he did. He lifted his gun and fired. Two thick blasts that were deafening.

They waited. Listening. There were no sounds of hurried footsteps. However, there was another shot from the gunman. This one smacked into the porch railing. Obviously, he knew where they were, and he'd given up on the windows. Now, he was going for the direct kill.

Daniel cursed again and used his forearm to cover her head. "Stay down," he whispered. "I'm going to try to get to the other side of the porch." He tipped his head in that direction. "I think I can drop down off the side and get to the cruiser."

"No." She couldn't say that fast enough. "That'd only make you an easy target." Kara had to pause a moment to gather her breath. "We'll both get to the other side of the porch," she suggested. "That'll put some distance between us and the shooter, and when we both drop down to the ground, we can run to the front where your brother's waiting. We'll have backup."

It was an awful plan, one that was filled with risks that could get them killed, but at the moment it was the only chance they had. If this shootout went on much longer, Barrett would likely storm in, and then he could be gunned down. They had to move fast.

And now.

"Come on," Kara insisted, shifting out from beneath Daniel. "Let's just hurry and do this."

She was counting on the gunman not having stellar marksmanship skills. Plus, Daniel and she would have the meager cover of the railing. She prayed both of those things would work in their favor.

"Let's go," Daniel said as soon as he got into a crouching position.

They did. Daniel and she scrambled across the porch. As expected, the shots came, one of them smacking into the railing and ricocheting off with a loud pinging sound of metal striking metal. Another hit the wood pillar on the corner of the porch. No glass this time, but instead they got hit with a spray of splinters.

The moment they were on the other side, Daniel and she dropped back down so they were flat on the porch. She could see better here, thanks to the illumination coming from the lights on Main Street. What she saw past the railing was a row of thick hedges where they'd need to jump, and the trick would be not to get tangled up in them.

Of course, first they had to get over the railing, which meant there'd be seconds where it'd be easier for the shooter to kill them.

"What the hell?" Daniel grumbled.

Kara's head snapped up, and she followed the direction of his gaze. Not toward the shooter. Or rather not from the area where the shooter had fired those last two shots. Daniel was looking at that Texas mountain laurel where earlier they'd seen the shadow.

But there was no shadow now.

No. This was a man. A man with blood on his shirt.

And staggering forward, he fell to the ground.

DANIEL FOUGHT HIS instinct to run to the man who'd just fallen, but he forced himself to stay back. Plus, he had to get Kara to a safer place, and that meant getting her off the porch.

"I want you to climb over the railing and drop down into the shrubs," Daniel told her, and he made sure it sounded like the order that it was. He didn't want her arguing about this, especially when he added, "I'll cover you."

Kara didn't argue, not verbally anyway, but he could see the hard questioning look she gave him. She might have continued that look, too, but the man lying in the yard moaned, and it was definitely the sound of someone in pain. He'd likely been shot. Could be dying. And Daniel couldn't get him the help he needed until he had Kara off this porch.

"Help me," the man said, his voice also laced with pain.

Well, maybe.

And maybe this was all just a trick to get them to go out into the open to check on him.

"Help me," he repeated, and Daniel could see the man struggling to crawl toward them.

He also saw the man's face.

Rizzo.

Daniel had no idea why Rizzo was there, but that blood probably wasn't part of the ruse—if there indeed was one. No. The blood was real, Daniel could smell it, and he could see it on the right sleeve and shoulder of Rizzo's shirt. The injury could have happened when someone kidnapped him and brought him here.

As bait.

If that was the plan, it wasn't going to work. Daniel couldn't *let* it work. He forced his attention back on the area where the gunman had last fired shots.

"Climb over the railing as fast as you can," he instructed Kara.

She certainly didn't jump to do that, and Daniel felt the hesitation coming off her in waves. "Just be careful," she finally said, and she got into a position to make the climb.

Daniel got in position, too. As best as he could, anyway. When she moved, so did he. He stood, took aim at where he presumed their attacker was, and he sent two shots in that direction. From the corner of his eye, he also kept watch of Rizzo. After all, the man could be armed and ready to strike.

Kara got over the railing fast, and Daniel released the breath he was holding when she dropped into the shrubs. Their attacker didn't fire, and Daniel didn't know if that was because he'd ducked or because he was on the move, looking for a better position so he could kill them.

Daniel scrambled over the railing right after her, landing directly in front of her. The shrubs poked and jabbed at the cuts they already had, but Daniel pushed aside the pain and focused.

"Keep watch behind us," he told Kara. He didn't think the gunman could get past Barrett to come at them from that way, but he couldn't take the risk.

"I need an ambulance," Rizzo muttered, still crawling toward Kara and him.

Yeah, he probably did need fast medical attention, but a wounded man could still be dangerous. He could still be a killer. However, Daniel had to rethink that theory when the gunman started shooting again. He'd moved and was now more in the back center of the yard, but Daniel couldn't see him. He could only see where the SOB was aiming.

At Rizzo.

Or at least he was aiming *near* Rizzo. Another shot blasted through the air. And another. Daniel couldn't be sure if either of the bullets had hit Rizzo, but if not, they were coming damn close. He couldn't just crouch there and let a man be murdered.

"Stay down," he warned Kara.

Daniel had to leave the meager cover of the shrubs so he could return fire. He sent what he hoped was three rounds into the shooter. Even if he didn't hit him, it caused him to stop long enough for Daniel to hurry out into the yard and take hold of Rizzo's uninjured arm. He began dragging the man to the shrubs.

And the gunman began firing again.

Daniel felt the searing pain from a bullet as it sliced across his own forearm. Cursing, he didn't let go of Rizzo, but he ducked down, trying to make himself less of a target.

The sound of the shots behind him caused an icy chill to ripple over Daniel's skin, and that chill only got colder when he realized that Kara was now out of the bushes and was trying to stop the gunman from doing any more damage. She was also putting herself right in the line of fire.

Daniel didn't bother to shout for her to get

down. She was focused on giving him precious seconds to get to safety. So that's what Daniel did. Still dragging Rizzo, he hurried to the side of the porch. Once they were by the shrubs, he let go of Rizzo, and in the same motion, he pulled Kara back to the ground.

Not a second too soon.

A bullet whipped through the air, cutting through the exact spot where she'd just been standing.

His life didn't exactly flash before his eyes, but it was close. Too close. And he felt a chill of a different kind. One that cut him all the way to the bone. He could have lost her.

Damn it, he could have lost her.

Later, he'd tell her that he hadn't wanted her to risk her life for his. Later, he'd tell her a lot of things. But for now, he just wanted to get her out of there.

Even with Rizzo's injuries and continued mumblings for help, Daniel frisked the man to make sure he couldn't pull a gun on them. But Rizzo wasn't armed. He also didn't seem to have any injuries other than the one to his shoulder, but there was so much blood that Daniel couldn't actually see the bullet wound.

"You're hurt," Kara said, her words rushing out with her breath.

Daniel glanced down at his arm and shook his head. "I'll be okay." He'd need stitches, but Rizzo's injury would also need some medical attention. "See what you can do to help Rizzo."

Kara kept hold of her gun, but she used her free hand to try to apply pressure to Rizzo's shoulder. Rizzo was writhing now, and his arms were flailing around, so she used her knees to pin his hands to the ground. As soon as she'd done that, however, the man went limp. For one terrifying moment, she thought he was dead, but she felt his pulse and realized he'd just passed out.

Daniel kept watch around them and took out his phone. He needed to text Barrett to see if he could pull a cruiser right into the side yard. That way, he could get both Kara and Rizzo into it so that Rizzo could be taken to the EMTs. But Daniel barely had time to take out his phone when something caught his eye.

A woman.

She came walking out of the shadows and into the yard.

"Don't shoot," she blurted out.

Daniel didn't, but he did take aim.

He didn't recognize the woman, a tall curvy brunette with her loose hair partially covering her face, but he could see that her hands were cuffed in front of her. There were also plastic restraints on the ankles of her bare feet.

And she wasn't alone.

Someone was behind her, using her as a human shield, and that someone had a gun pointed at her head.

"Don't shoot," the woman repeated, her voice shaking. She was shaking, too, and even in the darkness, Daniel could see that she was ghostly pale. "If you shoot, he'll kill me."

"He?" Daniel questioned.

Daniel heard her captor mutter something, but he couldn't make out what he'd said to her. Nor could he make out the voice. Was that Eldon or Sean behind the woman? Or was this someone else, maybe a henchman one of them had brought here to do his dirty work?

"Rizzo," she said. "He's the one who set all of this up."

Daniel glanced at the unconscious Rizzo. "Really?" He made sure her captor heard the skepticism in that one word.

There was more muttering. "Rizzo hired someone to scare Kara and you, to get you to back off the militia investigation. But Rizzo double-crossed him. Rizzo was going to kill the two of you and set up his hired gun to take all the blame."

Daniel tried to pick through the whirl of thoughts in his head to see if that made sense. Maybe. "What's the name of Rizzo's hired gun?" Daniel wanted to address the man and not talk through the hostage.

There were more mutterings, and the woman answered, "Ned."

Daniel seriously doubted that was the guy's real name, but it was a start. Now he needed more info fast. First, though, he handed Kara his phone and whispered for her to text Barrett.

"Who killed the surrogates?" Daniel asked. "Did you do that, *Ned*?"

"Rizzo killed them," she said without hesitating. "I'm Annie Cordova," she added a moment later.

Daniel hadn't recognized her face, but he sure as heck knew the name because he'd seen it on the list he'd gotten from the fertility clinic. She was another surrogate. And every instinct told him that she'd had no part in this attack, that she was just another innocent victim that a killer didn't mind using to get to Kara and him.

But who was using her?

Annie frantically shook her head at something that Ned told her, and the moonlight shimmered on the tears that spilled down her cheeks. “He said he’ll have to hurt me if you don’t swap places with me. He wants you to be his ticket out of here.”

“No,” Kara insisted. “It’s a trap.”

Probably. But maybe in Ned’s way of thinking, he’d have more to bargain with by using a cop instead of a surrogate. Of course, holding a cop was risky, too, because Daniel figured he was a much better bet at defending himself than Annie would be.

“You’re to toss your gun into the yard,” Annie went on. “And then step out. He’ll let me go when you do that.”

“Don’t. He’ll gun you down,” Kara warned him. Her voice was a raw tangle of fear and nerves, and she levered herself up enough to catch onto his arm as if to hold him back.

Daniel knew he didn’t have time to think this through. Ned wasn’t going to wait, especially not with other cops nearby, and Daniel couldn’t stand by and watch another woman die. However, he could make this harder for Ned, or whoever was behind Annie, to kill him.

“Give me your gun,” Daniel whispered to Kara.

“You’re not going out there,” Kara snapped. “You’re not going to sacrifice yourself. Promise me you won’t do that,” she added as she slipped him her weapon.

Daniel couldn't agree to that promise because he'd do whatever it took. He lowered his own gun to the side of his leg, and using his left hand, he tossed Kara's gun into the yard.

"I'm coming out," Daniel said the moment Kara's gun hit the ground. "Let go of Annie."

Daniel levered himself up just a little, his attention nailed to the surrogate. He made eye contact with her and tipped his head down. He hoped she got the message that he wanted her to drop. Once she was out of the way, then he'd be able to shoot the man holding her.

Annie gave a small nod back, and Daniel could see her steeling herself up to do what he'd silently asked.

But she didn't get the chance.

Her captor tossed Annie over his shoulder and started running. Before Daniel could do anything to stop him, they disappeared into the shadows. Even over the thudding of his own heartbeat, Daniel heard the sound of the man's running footsteps.

He was getting away.

"No!" Kara shouted before she could stop herself.

She knew it wouldn't do any good, that their attacker wasn't just going to turn himself in to be arrested, but the sheer frustration and dread had taken over. The gunman couldn't get away, especially not with a hostage. He just couldn't. Because if that happened, Daniel and she might never be safe.

They might never be able to bring Sadie home.

The killer could just wait until they thought they were in the clear and then come after them again. In the meantime, he would almost certainly kill Annie.

"Barrett?" Daniel called out to his brother. "I need you on the side of the porch with Kara."

Kara didn't have to ask why Daniel wanted that. He was going after the shooter. Part of her knew that had to happen, but the other part of her didn't want to risk losing him. She was in love with him. She would have told him that, too, but Barrett didn't waste any time getting to her. The moment he reached Rizzo and her, he gave Daniel the nod to get going.

Daniel did.

He hurried off into the night after the gunman and the hostage he'd taken.

She could have sworn her heart skipped several beats, and there was a pain in her chest because her muscles were too tense. Kara whispered a prayer and hoped that their attacker wasn't now lying in wait. Waiting to kill Daniel.

"Once Esther gets here, I'll give Daniel some backup," Barrett whispered to her.

With his gun drawn and his gaze firing all around them, Barrett positioned himself over Rizzo and her, obviously giving them protection in case the shooter circled back. If that happened, she wouldn't have a way to fight back since her gun was in the yard where Daniel had tossed it. She was considering whether or not to rush out and get it when she felt something.

Next to her, Rizzo groaned, and he reached down to rub his hand over his leg. "I think he shot me," he mumbled, his words barely coherent.

Kara couldn't see any blood there, but then it was dark so maybe she'd missed it. However, it wasn't dark enough for her to miss the glint of metal when Rizzo whipped out a gun from an ankle holster. Before Kara could even react, he had hold of her.

And he pointed the gun at her head.

For a few stunned moments, she didn't react. The shock of what was happening had left her frozen. Rizzo was behind this.

Rizzo was the one who wanted Daniel and her dead.

Kara didn't have to ask his motive. This was about revenge. This was his way of getting back at Daniel for his accusations about the militia, and that twisted her stomach into a knot. Daniel had just been doing his job, and now this monster was going to try to punish him for it.

By killing him.

By killing all those innocent surrogates.

If Rizzo had managed to get away with this, it would have looked as if Daniel's murder was tied to the surrogacy. To her. To the decision they'd made for her to carry Sadie.

She pushed aside the shock and fear and tried to ram her elbow into him, but Rizzo held on. Not easily. He was breathing hard, but she didn't think it was from pain. All of this had likely been some kind of ruse, and he could have put the blood on himself to make them believe he'd been shot.

Kara made a strangled sound, and she started to scramble away from them, but Rizzo stopped her by pressing the gun harder against her head.

"Move and you die," he told her before shifting his attention to Barrett. "You need to put down your weapon, Sheriff."

Barrett's eyes narrowed, and Kara knew he was doing the same thing she was—assessing the situation. Trying to figure a way out of this. It wouldn't be easy because Kara was literally between Rizzo and him.

She now knew the position of his body was intentional. So were the fake injury and his cry for help. Even pretending to be unconscious while he waited for the exact moment to strike was part of his plan. He'd set all of this up, including the weapon he'd drawn from the ankle holster. Rizzo had likely known that Daniel would frisk him, and he had, but they hadn't considered that Rizzo would have a concealed gun that he was now going to try to use to kill her.

"You know I can't do that," Barrett answered, his voice as icy as the glare he gave Rizzo. "If I put down my gun, you'll just kill all of us."

"Maybe. Maybe not." He might have tried to sound nonchalant, but he wasn't pulling it off. Kara heard the strain of nerves in his voice. Felt it in the knotted muscles of his arm.

"You don't need to do this," Kara tried.

Rizzo's response was a hollow laugh. "Right.

Let's just say I need to cover up the mess I made. I just need to wait a couple more minutes to make sure Ned takes care of Daniel."

Her stomach knotted even more. *Takes care of Daniel.* Ned was no doubt Rizzo's hired gun, and Rizzo had given him orders to kill Daniel.

"You killed all those surrogates," Kara managed to say. Maybe she could distract him. Or come up with some sort of diversion so that Barrett could get off a shot.

Rizzo certainly didn't deny committing the murders, nor was there any logic he could give her that would justify why he'd done that.

"You killed innocent women and attacked Daniel and me to cover up your own crimes," she snapped.

The sound of the gunshot stopped Kara from saying more. She felt the punch of dread, and she prayed that Daniel hadn't been on the receiving end of the bullet.

Oh, God.

Had Rizzo's henchman succeeded?

Was Daniel dead?

The thought of it was unbearable, and it sent a slam of rage into her. How dare this miserable excuse for a human being do such things. He had no right to put them in danger. And Kara used that rage, letting it build and soar until she had it pinpointed on the man behind her.

On a feral growl, she slammed her elbow into Rizzo, and in the same motion, Kara shoved away from him. Just in the nick of time. Rizzo pulled the trigger, and the bullet came so close to her that Kara could have sworn she felt the heat from it as it flew past her.

She punched him, trying to knock away the gun, but he fired again. The sound of it blasted through the night and merged with Barrett's shouts for her to get back.

But Kara couldn't get back from Rizzo. Nor could she run. If she did, Rizzo would be on her, and she seriously doubted he would have any reservations about shooting her in the back. No. He was basically a coward, preying on women who'd never done him a moment of harm.

Kara managed to latch onto Rizzo's right wrist, and she clamped on hard so she could try to keep his gun pointed away from Barrett and her. But Rizzo was a lot bigger and stronger than she was, and he'd obviously gotten his own slam of rage and adrenaline.

Barrett lunged toward them, ready to help, but Kara knew he didn't have a clean shot. Plus, Rizzo was using the positions of their bodies to his advantage. If Barrett tried to punch Rizzo, he could end up hitting her. While that wouldn't kill her, it might cause her to move the wrong way, and that could allow Rizzo to get off a shot.

"Put down the gun," someone shouted.

Daniel.

Kara couldn't see him, but there was no mistaking that voice, and she could also hear his running footsteps as he approached. The relief came, even stronger than her earlier rage. He was alive.

But he might not be for long.

From the corner of her eye, she could see Daniel running toward them, cutting through the smoke that had already made its way to the backyard. At the speed he was going, it wouldn't take him long to reach them, and Rizzo might be able to shoot him. Unlike some of his other shots, she doubted Rizzo would miss at such close range.

And Daniel could die.

Using brute force, Rizzo punched Kara with his left fist, and he hauled her to him so that Daniel wouldn't be able to shoot him. However, it would make Daniel an easy target for Rizzo. She couldn't just sit there and let Rizzo gun him down, especially when he was trying to save her.

Kara went at Rizzo again, and she managed to bash her elbow into his face. He cursed her, his growled tone a vicious threat. He turned and pivoted his hand.

So he could point his gun at her.

Kara had only a split second to decide what to do. Daniel was right there, already taking aim. Kara knew she had to move, too. So that Daniel would have the shot. So instead of trying to latch onto Rizzo again, she went limp and dropped on her side to the ground.

Time seemed to slow to a crawl, and she heard herself scream when Rizzo lifted his gun, pointing it right at Daniel. The blast came. A thick syrupy sound that quickly turned to an explosion in her head.

Rizzo had pulled the trigger.

Chapter Seventeen

Daniel didn't brace himself for Rizzo's shot. No time for that. He simply took aim as best he could and fired. Just as Rizzo did.

Rizzo missed.

Daniel didn't.

The shot slammed straight into Rizzo's chest, and Daniel heard the unmistakable sickening sound of the bullet tearing through him. Daniel hadn't meant for it to be a warning shot. That would have been too risky. So, he'd aimed to kill.

Rizzo's body went slack, his own gun sliding from a hand that was no longer receiving the right signals from his brain. Still, the man managed a dry smile.

"You'll never be able to save Annie," Rizzo said, attempting a grin. It was no doubt meant to taunt Daniel.

And it worked.

Because what Rizzo said could be the truth.

"Where's Annie?" Kara asked, her voice tight with the strain from the fear and the fight.

Daniel had to shake his head, and he glanced at Barrett. "Annie wasn't with the hired gun when I caught up to him. Either she got away or he stashed her somewhere."

Or he could have killed her.

Daniel hadn't heard the hired gun fire a shot, but he could have snapped her neck. However, Daniel didn't want Kara to have to deal with that possibility right now. Not when she looked to be barely hanging on by a thread.

"And the gunman, this *Ned*?" Barrett pressed, already getting to his feet.

Daniel tipped his head toward the area where he'd left him. "I had to shoot him, but he was alive when I cuffed him to the door of the dumpster behind the hardware store. He'll be able to tell you where Annie is."

Barrett volleyed a few glances at Kara, Rizzo and him, and his brother must have decided this situation here was under control because he took off running. Daniel heard him call someone, Esther probably, and he barked off orders for a search to find the now missing surrogate and to have the EMTs and the fire department move in. Daniel wished he could help, but there was no way he could leave Kara alone.

Struggling to get to her feet, she hurried to him, her gaze skimming over him, no doubt to check him for injuries. Daniel had a few, just cuts and bruises, but she had a lot more than he did. The nicks were still bleeding, and the right side of her face was swollen.

It felt like multiple punches to the gut to see her like that. To see the injuries that this SOB had caused, but Daniel didn't want Kara to feel his anger. He wanted to give her what comfort he could, so while keeping his gun aimed at Rizzo, he hooked his arm around her and pulled her to him for a hug. But he was the one who was comforted, and Daniel felt the immediate relief of just being able to hold her like this.

"Now, that's touching," Rizzo rasped out. He coughed, then groaned. "Guess you won this round, huh?"

Daniel thought it was a shame that Rizzo had used what little of his breath he had left for that. There'd been no confession. No remorse. Not even a message he wanted given to someone who might care for him. Just that stupid question that drilled home for Daniel just how senseless all the murders and violence had been.

Senseless enough that Kara had nearly died because of it.

Now, he watched Rizzo die. He heard the death rale, saw the life drain from the man's eyes. And Daniel felt both disgust and relief. Rizzo wouldn't be able to hurt another woman or launch another attack.

"We have to get away from the building," Daniel told Kara when he saw the firemen move in to start putting out the flames at the front of the inn. He also motioned to the two EMTs, and he pointed to Rizzo. "He's dead, but Kara needs help."

Kara was shaking her head before he even finished. "No. We have to look for Annie."

"Barrett will find Annie," he assured her, and Daniel hoped that was the truth.

He led her to the back of the ambulance, away from some of the smoke, away from Rizzo, and he had her sit while one of the EMTs started to examine those wounds on her face. The other EMT stooped down to take a look at Rizzo. Daniel stepped back so he could call Esther to see if she could give him an update on the search, but he spotted the deputy.

Not alone.

She was walking toward them, and she had the injured gunman in tow. The guy was bleeding, but he didn't appear to have any trouble walking. The man was definitely in better shape than Rizzo.

Daniel hurried toward them. So did one of the EMTs who'd been by Rizzo. "Did he say where he'd put Annie?" Daniel immediately asked.

He could tell from the deputy's expression that the answer to that was no. Daniel simply put out his hand to stop the EMT from going to the gunman. He didn't say that the piece of slime wouldn't get medical treatment until he talked, but Daniel was pretty sure he got his point across.

The gunman huffed. "I knocked her out and dumped her on the side of garbage bags in the alley."

Daniel texted that info to Barrett as fast as he could, and he instructed Esther to help Barrett with the search. Esther shoved the man to a sitting position on the ground and hurried off.

At the front of the inn, Daniel could hear the firemen getting to work. Maybe they'd be able to save the place. If not, it would end up being yet something else that Rizzo had ruined.

"I want a deal," the gunman insisted, giving

Daniel a snarling look. "I tell you everything you want to know about Rizzo, and I get immunity."

Not bothering to keep his language in check, Daniel told him what he could do with his immunity demand.

"You're not calling the shots here," Daniel reminded him. "You're going down for multiple murders, attempted murders, murders for hire, conspiracy, kidnapping and any other charge I can tack onto that. You'll be on death row before you know it."

Now it was the gunman who cursed. "I didn't kill anyone."

"Maybe not, but accessory to murder will still land you on death row."

Daniel finally saw something he wanted to see. The panic in the man's eyes. "I'm not going down for this," the gunman snapped. "Rizzo was the one who put all of this together."

Bingo. That was a good start, but Daniel wanted to hear a whole lot more. He glanced behind him to check on Kara—she was still being treated—and he gave the go-ahead nod to the other EMT to check the gunman's wounds.

"Keep talking," Daniel told the man as the

EMT stooped beside him. "Start with your name and don't stop until you've convinced me to take the death penalty off the table."

Something that Daniel doubted would happen even if the man told them everything. It didn't matter that he might not have actually killed anyone, accessory to murder carried the same penalty as murder itself.

"I'm Ned Kershaw," he finally said. "Rizzo and I belong...*belonged* to the same group."

"The militia," Daniel provided. "The Rangers have proof to put a stop to that." If they didn't already have that proof, they soon would with what he could get from this idiot.

"Yeah, but I can give the Rangers more. I can give the names of everyone in the group and the location of our stashes. I'll cooperate, and that should help cut back on my sentence."

Maybe, but that'd be up to the Rangers. It was possible they would indeed want to make a deal with him to take down a militia group. For now, though, Daniel was more interested in what Rizzo had done to the surrogates and what he'd tried to do to Kara and him.

"Tell me about Rizzo," Daniel demanded. "What was his part in all of this?"

Ned winced when the EMT cut away his shirtsleeve and began to clean the wound.

"Rizzo set all of this up," Ned repeated. "He killed those women. The surrogates from that clinic. He figured that way when he killed you and your woman, that he wouldn't get the blame, that the crazy guy who lost his daughter would."

Daniel shook his head. "Rizzo was going to set up this man to make him look guilty?"

"Yeah," Ned confirmed. "Rizzo sent him some pictures to stir him up. Said he was already right on the edge since he was all broken up about losing his daughter. Rizzo thought maybe the crazy guy would do the job for him, that he'd kill you because it'd look like you were trying to set him up. But the crazy guy didn't take the bait. That's when Rizzo tried to stir up the other guy, too, by shooting him."

Sean. So that explained who'd shot Sean and why.

"Rizzo didn't want this second man dead?" Daniel pressed.

"No. The idea was for him to go after you and your woman. He was one pissed off guy, I gotta tell you, and Rizzo thought he wouldn't have to push him too much. Still, I guess he didn't push fast enough 'cause Rizzo set all of this up."

Ned was right about Sean's anger level. He

was indeed a hothead. But obviously Rizzo hadn't been able to provoke him into committing murder.

"I didn't know about any of that, though, about shooting that man until after it was a done deal," Ned went on a moment later. "When things didn't go the way Rizzo wanted at the hospital, he hired me to help him tonight. All I was supposed to do was hold the other woman. Annie," he clarified. "And I was to fire shots that didn't hit anybody. Especially Rizzo."

Daniel could see Rizzo setting up something like this, but there was one piece that didn't fit. And it was a huge piece. "Why didn't Rizzo just have you gun me down when you had the chance?" He could have easily done that when Daniel had stood to toss Kara's gun into the yard.

"Because he wanted to do it himself," Ned answered without a moment's hesitation. "He said no one but him was gonna put a bullet in you and that he wanted you to watch while he killed your woman."

None of that was a surprise, but hearing it still packed a wallop. Daniel saw that same reaction in Kara's eyes when she walked toward him and stood by him. She touched his arm, and he was surprised at how much that simple gesture steadied him. Actually, everything about her steadied him, but Daniel knew they had a long road ahead of them. It was going to take a lifetime or two to get past the nightmare that Rizzo had created.

"How'd Rizzo ever expect to get away with this?" Kara asked.

"He faked being shot when he fell in the yard," Ned explained while the EMT worked on him. "He had some of his own blood drawn, and he used that. He said that would have been on all your clothes when your bodies were found. He'd planned on putting it on the crazy man's clothes, too. So, when Rizzo just disappeared, it'd look like the crazy man had also killed him."

Rizzo had obviously planned on running. On making a new life somewhere else. A life that wouldn't have involved any jail time for his involvement with the militia or all the murders he'd committed. A life where Kara, he and anyone else who'd gotten in Rizzo's way would have been dead.

Since Ned was still wearing his cuffs, Daniel risked taking his attention off the man for a couple of seconds so he could pull Kara into his arms. She was trembling, probably dealing with an adrenaline crash, but she still looked better than she had a couple of minutes ago. That was in part because the EMT had wiped most of the blood off her face, but Daniel could see the relief there, too. Rizzo was dead. The threat to Sadie was over.

He looked down at her, their gazes connecting, and Daniel realized there was so much he wanted to say to her. Things that would have to wait, though, he realized, because she spoke first.

"I'm in love with you," she blurted out. "And I know the timing sucks for telling you that, but after everything that just happened, I didn't want to wait another minute without telling you."

Daniel just stared at her. He certainly hadn't seen this coming. But he knew it was true. She was in love with him. He also knew she was right about the timing being bad, and his response was going to have to wait. That's because he caught the motion out of the corner of his eye.

Since his body was still on alert, he pushed Kara behind him and pivoted in that direction. However, there was no need for him to take aim. It was Barrett.

And he had Annie with him.

"She's okay," Barrett quickly assured them, and he handed the woman off to an EMT who came rushing toward them.

"He bashed me on the head with his gun," Annie snapped. She sounded more riled than hurt, and she aimed a nasty glare at Ned. "I hope you put him in jail and throw away the key."

Daniel thought that was a stellar idea. He wanted the man in a cage and was certain that's exactly where he'd be.

"She needs to go to the hospital," one of the EMTs said, referring to Annie. He looked at Kara and Daniel. "You two do, as well. You're both pretty cut up, and you're going to need some stitches."

Stitches weren't a picnic, but Daniel thought they were a small price he was willing to pay, considering their injuries could have been much, much worse.

"Go ahead to the hospital," Barrett told them. "All three of you can go in the ambulance, and Esther and I will take care of things here."

Daniel hated to put all of this on his brother and his fellow deputy, but he doubted Kara would go to the hospital without him. That's why he slipped his arm around her and began to lead her to the ambulance that was parked behind the fire truck.

"After the hospital, we'll go see Sadie," Daniel assured her.

That made her smile, and he wasn't sure how she managed to look so darn good when they'd both been beat to hell and back. But she did. Kara looked amazing. So amazing that he couldn't stop himself from leaning down and brushing a kiss on her mouth.

"I'd like that," Kara whispered. She kissed him, too. It was both casual and intimate, the kind of kiss that couples shared even after they'd been together for years. "I like this."

He knew what she meant. *This* was those kisses. Him, holding on to her. Them being together even if it was only for this moment. For this night.

Or longer.

Kara clearly wanted *this* to last for a while. And that was something they needed to discuss. Maybe when they got to the hospital, he could find a minute to talk to her alone so he could ask her about what she'd said to him.

I'm in love with you.

He'd heard the words clearly enough, but Daniel wasn't sure she'd meant them. No. Her emotions had been sky-high, and coupling the danger with the fact they'd had sex must have made her believe her feelings went beyond…

Daniel stopped. Literally and mentally.

With the EMTs and Annie ahead of them, Daniel looked down at Kara. "It's been a tough night," he said, testing the waters. Or something. Heck, he wasn't sure what he was doing, but he suddenly felt off-kilter.

No.

That wasn't it.

He suddenly felt as if everything was…right.

"You're in love with me?" He hadn't intended for that to be a question or for him to make it sound as if it were some kind of miracle. But it was. It fit the miracle label just fine.

"I am." She didn't smile this time, but there seemed to be a contentment about her when she looked into his eyes. "How much of a problem will that be for you?"

Daniel had heard a lot of tough things tonight, including some tough questions. But that wasn't one of them.

"No problem at all," he assured her—after he kissed her again.

This time, though, it was a lot more than a brush of his lips on hers. He made sure that she felt it. Hopefully all the way to her toes.

It must have worked because when he pulled back, she had a dreamy smile on her face.

"Good," she whispered. "Because I plan to love Sadie and you for a long, long time."

Since that was exactly what Daniel had in mind, he smiled, too, and kissed Kara again. Soon, very soon, he wanted to get started on that long, long time.

* * * * *

Look for more books in
USA TODAY *bestselling*
author Delores Fossen's
Mercy Ridge Lawmen miniseries,
coming soon.

And don't miss the first book in the series:

Her Child to Protect

Available now wherever
Harlequin Intrigue books are sold!